"Strip down."

Zach sighed, thinking it was just his luck to have been sprayed by a family of skunks—and in front of a sexy woman. Even though he had no qualms about shedding his clothes, he said, "Turn around."

Sunny shot him a droll look, then turned. "Are you done yet?" she asked after a long moment. "I want to get back to town."

"Lest you forget, I'm naked. Got anything I could wear?"

She chuckled. "Nothing. Surely you've got something in your truck."

"A chamois cloth."

"Well, get it."

Zach glared at her turned back. Was he really going to ride into town with her…wearing a chamois cloth as a loincloth? Suddenly he gulped. He was about to be caught with his pants down—and with the town's favorite belle. With the luck he was having, he'd wind up at an altar with a shotgun at his back!

ABOUT THE AUTHOR

Cathy Gillen Thacker is a full-time novelist who once taught piano to children. Born and raised in Ohio, she attended Miami University. After moving cross-country several times, she settled in Texas with her husband and three children.

Books by Cathy Gillen Thacker

Cathy Gillen Thacker

A SHOTGUN WEDDING

Harlequin Books

TORONTO • NEW YORK • LONDON
AMSTERDAM • PARIS • SYDNEY • HAMBURG
STOCKHOLM • ATHENS • TOKYO • MILAN
MADRID • WARSAW • BUDAPEST • AUCKLAND

ISBN 0-373-16587-0

A SHOTGUN WEDDING

Copyright © 1995 by Cathy Gillen Thacker.

This edition published by arrangement with Harlequin Enterprises B.V.

® and TM are trademarks of the publisher. Trademarks indicated with ® are registered in the United States Patent and Trademark Office, the Canadian Trade Marks Office and in other countries.

Printed in U.S.A.

Prologue

Here Comes Temptation

She was a vision, with her angel's face and her glorious mane of curly hair streaming down her back and gleaming red-gold in the sunshine. Her slender curves were encased in knee-length khaki hiking shorts, a powder blue-tan-and-white plaid shirt and powder blue vest. Thick white knee socks came halfway up her long, spectacular legs. Serious hiking boots were on her incredibly dainty-looking feet.

Not ready to leave his unexpected find just yet, Zach braked his truck and paused for a second leisurely look.

A backpack slung over one shoulder, the angel in the meadow resembled a classy ad for ultraexpensive camping gear. The only exception in the picture of beautiful woman and nature at its alluring best was the clipboard and pen in her hands. She appeared to be writing something down as she went from tender sapling to sapling, moving among the wildflower-strung Tennessee property with unexpected grace.

Unfortunately, Zach thought with a frown as he took in the rest of her surroundings, he wasn't the only one who had noticed the pretty lady, and he was quite sure she had no idea she was being followed. Since he was the only other person within miles of the rural mountain property, he figured it was up to him to warn her. Scowling at the potentially risky nature of his mission, he steered his pickup to the side of the narrow country road, parked and got out. He shut the door quietly, then moved around the front of the truck.

The angel had her back to him. She was busy checking out leaves and scribbling on the clipboard in front of her.

For safety's sake, Zach decided to head north of her. He hopped the fence stealthily, giving the pending disaster wide berth, then moved to the north. He wished he could just shout, tell her not to move, but a call from him was liable to startle her, and given what was at stake—for both of them now—he didn't want to chance it.

His strides long and easy, he closed the distance between the woman and him. Behind her, to Zach's growing chagrin, disaster closed in, too. He was already beginning to regret his gallant actions. Doing his best to blend in with the environment, he whistled "Bob-white, Bob-white."

To his frustration, the angel didn't look up.

So much for ye olde Mother Nature approach. Zach reached into his pocket. He withdrew a dime. Aiming carefully, he tossed it at her shoulder. It hit her, bounced off and fell to the ground. She frowned and rubbed her arm without even looking up from the tree she was examining.

Zach swore softly. The woman was right in the middle of disaster and she was too absorbed in whatever she was doing even to realize it.

Knowing speed was of the essence now, he withdrew a quarter and aimed this coin at her clipboard. It bounced off the paper. She glanced up in alarm, stepped back quickly, saw Zach and let out a piercing yelp of surprise.

''Don't move!' he mouthed silently, letting his eyes convey the immediate physical danger she was in. But it was too late; her assailant was already zipping into action. Heart pounding, Zach knew there was only one thing to do. He called upon his years of high-school football, dashed in and grabbed the angel about the middle. To his chagrin, they were both hit with gargantuan force, even as he knocked her aside. Teeth clenched, Zach swore like a longshoreman. His first job in Carlisle was more than he bargained for.

Chapter One

You Done Me Wrong (And That Ain't Right)

"Arrggh!' Sunny Carlisle screamed as the horrible skunk spray assaulted her with hurricane force. Choking on the tear-gaslike fumes, she extricated herself from the big stupid oaf who had tackled her and stumbled to her feet. Dimly aware that he was yelling, coughing and choking, too, she grabbed her backpack and clipboard and headed for the ice-cold mountain stream at a run. She had to get this stuff off of her!

She reached the stream first. Without a glance at the hopelessly inept good Samaritan behind her, she dumped her gear on the bank, waded blindly in up to her waist and then knelt to submerge herself to her shoulders.

He came in right after. "Sorry about that," he apologized, right before he went under. He came up, his ash blond hair slicked back, his face all red from the fumes. After several more dunkings, he introduced himself. "I'm Zach Grainger."

"I'm Sunny Carlisle," she sputtered grimly, barely able to believe she was in such a predicament. "And if I didn't know better, I'd think you were yet another decoy sent to distract me," she muttered. After all, she huffed angrily to herself, the other interlude had started out almost exactly like this—minus the misguided attempt at heroism, of course.

"What are you talking about?" Zach demanded, flinging the water from his face.

"My parents. Do they know you're here?" It was possible they'd found out Zach was coming and had bought him off, too. She knew they hadn't given up getting her out of Carlisle altogether.

To his credit, though, Zach looked thoroughly confused.

"Who are your parents?"

"Elanore and Eli Carlisle."

"Sorry, I haven't met them. Yet, anyway." He paused. "Should I have?"

"No!" Sunny said. She studied Zach Grainger a moment longer. He seemed to be telling the truth. And given that he'd been born and raised in Tennessee, unlike her, there was little chance he'd ever met her parents, never mind agreed to one of their well-meant schemes. She was just overreacting, she assured herself boldly, because of what had happened before. Deliberately Sunny pushed her past romance and the humiliation she'd suffered at the hands of her ex-fiancé from her mind.

Still a little befuddled, Zach watched as she washed herself vigorously through her clothes, then followed suit, scrubbing uselessly at his own shirt and jeans. To Sunny's chagrin, they both smelled to high heaven and looked even worse. Realizing they were both using up tremendous energy with little result, she stopped what she was doing and glared at him. "I can't believe this," she muttered to no one in particular. "My life has turned into an episode of 'I Love Lucy'!"

He reacted defensively. "Well, so has mine, and don't stare at me like that," he counseled sternly. "I was trying to do you a favor by alerting you to the danger you were in!"

Well, that made all the difference. "Some favor. You got us both sprayed," Sunny grumbled, trying hard not to notice how devastatingly handsome Zach Grainger was in person. The black-and-white photo he'd sent in with his application did not convey the windblown appeal of his straight ash blond hair, long-lashed blue eyes, athletic build and all-American face. He was sexy in a very clean-cut, outdoorsy way.

"How long is it going to take for the skunk smell to go away?" Zach asked.

Sunny sighed pragmatically and tried to compose herself. "It won't. It's on our clothes. We'll have to burn them."

"What about us?" he inquired dryly. "We can't exactly set fire to ourselves, can we?"

Actually, Sunny thought, he had already done that to her senses, first with the tackle and then when he'd given her the once-over, but he didn't need to know she had personally reviewed and approved his application for employment. "No, I guess we can't," she said sagely. She gave him a brisk, purposeful smile.

"So what are we going to do next?" he asked.

Good question. "We're in luck. I have a can of vegetable juice in my backpack."

"What good will that do?"

"Boy, you are a greenhorn, aren't you?"

"Give me a break. I'm a complete novice when it comes to skunks."

"How well I know that."

"I'm also the new physician for the area."

"I know that, too," Sunny retorted, and then wished she hadn't.

Zach edged closer, his brawny shoulder temptingly near.

"How do you know that?"

Sunny paused uncomfortably as she tore her eyes from the broad, muscular planes of his chest, beginning to feel a little guilty, although there was no reason she should, she told herself stubbornly. Her part in bringing Zach to Carlisle had been completely aboveboard. "Carlisle is a small town, with a population of just 317."

Deciding they were standing much too close, Sunny stepped back. "Although they'll be changing the sign to 318 if you plan on staying."

Zach shrugged and kept his eyes on hers. "I don't really have much choice, since this is where the state assigned me to go," he said. He regarded her curiously. "Are there many people our age in Carlisle?" he asked.

Again Sunny had a tinge of regret. This was something she felt Zach should have been told up front. The other people on the selection committee had disagreed with her, and the majority vote had won out.

"Actually, there are very few people our age in the area," Sunny admitted. "Almost none of them single. So it can be hell trying to find someone to date."

That was one of the few serious drawbacks to living in the small Tennessee mountain town. But to Sunny, it was a manageable situation, at least for the time being. Since her failed engagement six months earlier, she hadn't wanted to date.

"I assume you live in Carlisle, also."

"Yes, I work there, too."

Zach tilted his head and studied her silently. "You any relation to the Carlisle Furniture Factory?"

Sunny nodded, unable to prevent her pride from bubbling forth. "I run it—for my grandfather."

Zach nodded, impressed. "So what do you do for entertainment on Saturday nights?" he asked, after glancing at her left hand and seeing no wedding ring.

"Usually I work."

"Oh." Zach felt a little disappointed.

Deciding they'd chatted long enough, Sunny began to unbutton her shirtsleeves. Zach turned his back to her. "I suppose you've got a spare set of clothes in that backpack," he said hopefully.

"Unfortunately," Sunny said tightly, "no." She was just going to have to make do. Determined to get on with this and do what absolutely had to be done, she tore off her clothes and hurled them into the bushes one by one. Then she popped open the can of vegetable juice. Using the hem of her bandanna, she saturated it with the juice and began rubbing it all over her body.

"Are you sure you should be doing this here and now?" Zach asked, glancing over his shoulder in the opposite direction, toward the road. "I mean, what if someone comes by?"

Sunny blew out a breath. "We've already established who you are and that you're a gentleman, if a novice at living in the country and knowing how to properly handle skunks. Besides, one false move and I'll hit you with the pepper spray I've got in my backpack."

Zach sighed. "If only you had used that on the mother skunk first," he lamented.

"I might've, had you given me a proper signal so that I'd known she was there."

"I tried. I whistled."

"Well, I didn't—wait a minute." Sunny paused and did a double take. "You did the Bob-white thing?"

"Yes."

"That was pretty good," Sunny admitted reluctantly. "So good, in fact, that I paid no attention to it. You should have tried some other kind of whistle."

"Such as?"

"I don't know." Sunny noticed the back of Zach was every bit as sexy and enticing as his front. "You could have whistled a country song."

Zach swept his hands through his hair, the muscles in his back rippling as he moved. "I'm not that good a whistler. I can only manage a couple of notes."

Sunny watched as he began to slowly unbutton his drenched cotton shirt. "I bet you could have fired off a wolf whistle, though," Sunny countered.

Zach did not deny experience in that regard. "Good point."

Sunny became unaccountably aggravated again. "Yeah, well, remember it next time," she muttered, just loud enough for him to hear.

"Believe me, I will," Zach muttered back, mocking her cantankerous tone.

Silence fell between them. Sunny finished scrubbing herself from head to toe. She'd need to soak in a tub of vegetable juice before the skunk smell dissipated. But at least it was to the point where her eyes were no longer burning and she was able to breathe without coughing and choking.

She set the half can of precious juice aside and ripped a red-and-white checkered tablecloth from her backpack, then began to dress. Already the sun was beginning to set. Thank goodness. They could head back to town under the cover of darkness. And then this whole sorry episode would be over. "Okay," she said, "your turn."

ZACH SWIVELED AROUND. Sunny Carlisle was up on the bank above him. She had a red-and-white checkered tablecloth wrapped around her, toga-style, and secured in a knot behind her neck. She still had her hiking boots on. Her glorious hair was streaming over her shoulders in a mass of thick curls that, when wet, looked dark red.

"Strip down and use the vegetable juice all over you," Sunny instructed calmly. "The tomato juice in it will help neutralize the smell. Then we'll head back to town."

Zach had no qualms about stripping in front of a woman, but he decided to have a little fun with Sunny. He grinned at her, glad he was not in the market for romance. "Turn your back first."

Sunny shot a droll look at him, then turned around. Zach kept his eyes on her as he hurled his clothes into the bushes on the opposite bank, just as she had done. Damn, but she was beautiful. Feisty, too. But she appeared awfully young and somehow *innocent* beneath her sage country ways. "How old are you anyway?" Zach asked, as he climbed down from the bank and kicked off his soggy tennis shoes. Naked, he began rubbing the juice all over him, savoring every drop.

"Twenty-four. How old are you?"

They weren't so far apart in age after all. "Twenty-nine."

Sunny peered at him from beneath a fringe of red-gold lashes. "Why did you want to know how old I am?" she asked.

"I just wondered." Zach shrugged. "You seem a little young to be running a factory."

"I'm old enough," she said. "Are you done yet? I want to get back to town."

Zach emptied the can. "Unless you've forgotten," he deadpanned, "I'm still buck naked. What have you got in that backpack of yours that I can wear?"

"Nothing," Sunny said. "Surely you have something in your pickup truck," she insisted blithely.

"A chamois." A used one, Zach thought grimly.

She made a sweeping gesture in the direction of his pickup. "Have at it, then."

"Sunny, you *want* me to run buck naked through that field over to my truck," Zach drawled.

"Want to borrow my clipboard?"

"What if someone drives by and sees us together?"

Sunny shrugged, unconcerned. "No one has yet."

Nothing seemed to bother Miss Carlisle, Zach thought.

"What were you doing out here today anyway?" Sunny asked.

"I got here a few hours ago. I dumped my gear at the clinic and decided to go for a drive to see the countryside." And that decision had led to his introduction to the angel with the feisty spirit. Zach grinned. Life in Carlisle was definitely looking up.

"WHAT DO YOU MEAN we can't ride in your pickup?"

Sunny asked ten minutes later, as she and Zach rejoined each other and squared off next to his shiny new truck.

In hiking boots and a tablecloth, she knew she looked ridiculous. He didn't look much better in that soft clinging chamois. She had expected him to put in on diaper-style or something. Instead he had ripped it in two, torn off a strip and secured it like a loincloth around his waist. It dipped just low enough to allow him some modesty, but not much, and made him look like one of the warriors in *Last of the Mohicans*. All tanned, muscular and so very male. Just seeing him made her pulse jump.

"Zach, we have to take your truck," Sunny continued. It was beginning to get dark.

"We still smell pretty bad." Hands on his hips, he leaned down so he and Sunny were nose to nose. "Or hadn't you noticed?"

"I know how we smell," Sunny said, exasperated. She stepped back and waved her arms at him. "That's why I want to go home. So I can soak in a tub of pure tomato juice."

Zach regarded her with all the sensitivity of a rock.

"Well, we're not getting into my truck smelling this way," he said firmly, carefully extracting a flashlight from the glove compartment and then locking his vehicle up tight as a drum. "This truck is brand-new and I'll be damned if I'm going to see it ruined with the aroma of skunk."

Sunny folded her arms in front of her. "You're being ridiculous," she fumed.

Zach gave her a complacent smile. "I may be a greenhorn, but I know how long the smell of skunk lingers wherever it's sprayed. Besides, I don't see you offering your vehicle," Zach continued irascibly.

"That's because my Land Rover is parked another two miles from here on an old logging road," Sunny said hotly.

Zach shrugged his broad shoulders uncaringly. "So let's start walking," he suggested.

It did not appear Sunny had any choice. Her mood souring even more, she fell into step beside him and hoped for the best.

"Isn't there a house near here?" Zach said after a while, as they kept to the other side of the ditch and followed the road.

"Nope. We're on company land."

His brow furrowed. He turned toward her slightly. "I thought Carlisle Furniture Factory was on the other side of town."

"It is. We grow the trees for the furniture here."

"Is that what you were doing today? Checking out trees?"

Sunny nodded. "We replant at three times the rate we harvest, but we're thinking of upping that to maybe five times if the land will support it."

"You really know your business," Zach said, looking a bit surprised.

"It's my job to know about reforestation," Sunny said as they approached her vehicle. Like his truck, her Land Rover was brand-new and sported four-wheel drive. She unlocked the door and climbed in. Tossed her gear in back.

Zach studied the pristine interior. He was feeling a little guilty about not using his truck. "You're sure about this?" he said. "You know, we could just keep walking. It's only another five or six miles to town."

Sunny shook her head. "The later it gets, the more likely we'll run into traffic on this road. The kids come from miles around to park out here. The sheriff drives by on a regular basis to catch them."

Zach groaned. That was all he needed. Because they had no choice, they both got in. Zach arranged his loincloth to give him maximum coverage and folded his arms in front of him. He felt ridiculous.

Sunny drove toward town. "What time is it?" she asked after a while.

Zach looked at his watch. "Nine o'clock."

She scowled. "Damn, that's awfully early."

"Drive by the clinic. I'll see if I can sneak in."

Sunny tightened her hands on the steering wheel. "The clinic is on Main Street!"

"So drive around the back," Zach suggested affably, his gaze discreetly following the movement of one sensationally curved leg from accelerator, to brake and then back again.

"No." Sunny blushed at just the thought of being seen like this. "No way. Not with streetlights. I'm not going to be seen driving you around town like this.

We'll just have to go to my house, over on Maple Street, sneak in the back and wait until later to drop you at the clinic.''

"Fine, whatever." Zach was really at his breaking point. Every time she moved, he could see the fluidness of her breasts beneath the thin cotton cloth, a more revealing slip of thigh.

"Do you think it's hot in here?" He rolled down his window a little more.

"I think it's freezing."

Zach glanced at her. He could see that, too. She had goose bumps everywhere.

They hit the edge of town. "Oh, damn, here comes another car. Get down!" Sunny said. As Zach bent out of sight, she turned off on a side street.

Finally the Land Rover stopped. Zach stayed where he was. His face just inches from the soft skin of Sunny's knee, he wondered what kind of perfume she wore. The prospect of finding out conjured up many exciting thoughts.

"We're here," Sunny whispered, relief quavering in her voice.

Reluctantly Zach straightened and moved away from her soft knee. He looked at the small, neat, two-story red brick house with the ornate white gingerbread trim and glossy pine green shutters. Leafy trees and neatly kept flower beds inundated the yard. A stand-alone garage in matching red brick was behind the house, at the end of a long drive.

"We're going in the back," Sunny said. "And don't slam your door," she commanded.

They crept out of her Land Rover. In the distance, a dog barked. The sounds of a television floated out from an open window across the street. Sunny moved stealthily from the cover of a shade tree, to a lilac bush, to the back door. Zach followed. She was fumbling with the lock, when another car hit the drive.

Sunny swore and dropped her keys. "Duck!" she ordered. "Maybe whoever it is won't see us!" Too late. They were caught in the headlights of a sedan. She swore and slowly straightened as the motor died and a car door opened.

Grimacing his displeasure, Zach straightened, too. He wasn't pleased to be in this situation, but he figured he might as well face it like a man.

"What in tarnation is going on here?" a raspy voice demanded.

The voice belonged to a tall, fit man in his early sixties. He had short red-gold hair that was laced with gray, piercing whiskey-colored eyes and a familial resemblance to Sunny Carlisle that was unmistakable. He carried a shotgun in his hand.

Sunny blanched. "What are you doing here, Gramps?"

"You were supposed to meet me for dinner tonight, remember? When you didn't show up or call, I knew something must be wrong. I called the police station to let them know there might be trouble and came out looking for you." He eyed Sunny sternly. "I can see it's a good thing I did, too."

"Now, Gramps, I can explain all this!" Sunny admonished with a nervous little laugh. "It's all quite amusin—oh, no!" She moaned as a second car pulled in her drive.

Two patrolmen jumped out, their guns drawn, and ran toward Sunny and Zach. "We got here as fast as we could, Mr. Carlisle!'' one of them yelled. "What the heck—''

The other cop stopped short as he got a good look at Sunny and her tablecloth.

"We got hit by skunk spray,'' Sunny said to one and all.

"I can smell that,'' Gramps admitted grimly. "The question is," he continued, glaring at Zach, his distrust evident, "what were *you* doing when the two of you got hit?''

Zach had learned in medical school that there were some people you just didn't mess with, particularly when they were upset. Augustus Carlisle was apparently one of them. He was not only the town mayor and the owner of the largest business in town, but his company was paying half Zach's salary, with the state and the community picking up the other portion. Keeping his hands high in a gesture of surrender, Zach said calmly, "I was trying to warn Miss Carlisle that she was about to get sprayed.''

"As you can smell, we got sprayed anyway,'' Sunny said. "We had to ditch our clothes, since they bore the heaviest concentration.''

"You sure you're okay, Miss Carlisle?'' the patrolman asked. When she nodded, he and his partner holstered their guns.

Zach could see Sunny's grandfather was still very upset. He looked at the patrolmen. "Perhaps you guys could give me a ride back to my clinic?''

"Sure thing,'' one of them said.

Gramps held up a hand to stop him. "I'll admit the young fella needs some clothes. As for the rest...''

Gramps looked at Sunny deliberately, then continued in a stern, determined tone as he picked up the shotgun and pointed it at Zach, "There's only one way to handle this!"

Chapter Two

Stand By Your Man

"I have this friend who's been having some chest pains every now and again," Augustus Carlisle began the moment he walked into the clinic.

Dressed in fishing gear, the scent of lakewater clinging to his clothes, Gramps made it appear as if his were a casual visit. Zach knew it was anything but.

"My question is, Doc, how would this friend of mine know the difference between ordinary chest pains that come from getting older versus those generated by something serious like a heart attack about to happen?"

"It depends." Zach sat down in a waiting-room chair. "Is your friend having any numbness or tingling with these chest pains of his? Any loss of consciousness?"

"No, not so far," Gramps said carefully, fingering one of the intricate fishing lures he had pinned to his vest. His eyes glowed with relief. "Does this mean my friend is off the hook as far as his heart goes?"

"Not necessarily. Those chest pains could be early warning signs of heart trouble. Then again, they could just as easily be something else, too. If I were you I'd advise your friend to get a physical. And speaking of physicals, when was the last time you had one, Augustus?"

"Never you mind." He shook a finger at Zach. "You worry about my granddaughter. I'll see to my health." Gramps took off in a huff.

No sooner had he driven off than Sunny walked in. The warm spring wind had tossed her red-gold hair into sexy disarray. Sunshine added color to her cheeks. But she was dressed for business, in a trim navy suit that clung to her slender curves.

"What was that all about?" she asked a little breathlessly, flattening one hand over the jewel neckline of her white silk blouse.

"I'm not sure," Zach frowned. He eyed Sunny. "What's up with you?" She sure looked pretty today, sexy in an unconscious way.

"The same." Sunny dropped her handbag into a chair. "Everyone thinks I should marry you."

"Only one problem," Zach said dryly, ignoring the mysteriously determined sparkle in her whiskey-colored eyes. "I haven't asked."

Sunny leveled a gaze at him as she dropped into a chair with a sigh. "Under the circumstances, Zach, maybe you should."

LONG MOMENTS LATER, Zach was still regarding Sunny incredulously. "This is nuts," he said as he paced the empty waiting room restlessly.

"My parents would agree with you, I'm sure," Sunny murmured. "Fortunately, I am not planning to tell them about our marriage until it's legal, so we don't have to worry about them interfering."

Zach pushed the edges of his starched white lab coat back, revealing a pin-striped blue-and-white dress shirt, matching tie and jeans. "Listen, Sunny, I think you're a great gal, but I won't marry you! I don't care how we were undressed or dressed the night we met."

Sunny glared at Zach. "You think I want to go through with this?" She plastered a hand across her chest, aware she only had thirty-three minutes of her lunch hour left. "You think I want my reputation besmirched?"

Zach couldn't believe the town was making such a big deal out of an innocent situation. He sank down on the vinyl sofa beside her. "People have actually been giving you a hard time?"

Silence fell in the room as they measured each other. "Everyone feels sorry for me...but wants to kill you."

"I know." Zach swept a hand through his hair. "For some crazy reason they think I took advantage of you."

Sunny rolled her eyes. What an understatement that was. She smiled at him consolingly. "I know you were only trying to help me." Unfortunately, that didn't change things.

"So now what?" Zach asked wearily.

Remembering she had brought them both lunch, Sunny opened the brown paper bag by her side and pulled out two containers of frozen strawberry yogurt. She handed Zach a container and plastic spoon, then popped hers open.

"I can't go on like this. I thought—hoped it would get better if we just stayed away from each other, but it's been two weeks now." She had neither seen nor spoken to Zach, yet he had never been very far from her mind. There was just something about him that made her heart race. "And nothing has changed."

"I know." Zach considered her a moment.

"And I understand it's been worse for you," Sunny sympathized.

He nodded grimly. "Not a single patient has come to see me. I've been open two weeks, and they're still driving sixty-five miles to see another doctor."

"That really upsets you, doesn't it?"

"The success of my first assignment means everything to my future."

"Has anyone even made an appointment?"

"Your grandfather stopped by to inquire about a friend who might need medical attention. And I advised his friend to get a checkup," Zach replied. If indeed Gramps had been talking about a friend.

"I guess everyone else must still be driving sixty-five miles to see another doctor," Sunny said dispiritedly, feeling all the more responsible for the predicament Zach was in.

"And all because I refused to marry you, even at the end of the gun."

"I admit Gramps can be a little dramatic," Sunny conceded dryly.

"A little?" Zach echoed, the first hint of humor curling his lips. He studied Sunny with great care. "I thought he was going to shoot me right on the spot."

The scene on her porch that night had been right out of a Li'l Abner comic strip, Sunny thought. But the dramatic effect it and the resulting community concern had worked on her life was all too real. "I hate to suggest it, but maybe we really should get married," Sunny said reasonably, adding, "just for a little while." It would quiet gossip and get Zach off the hook. And it would teach her parents a lesson and perhaps head off any further matchmaking schemes on their part. She kept expecting them to turn up with another prospective beau.

Zach's expression grew stony with resolve. His amiable mood vanishing, he set down his frozen yogurt with a thud and vaulted off the couch. He stared out the window at the sparse traffic on Main Street, his expression unaccountably dark and brooding. "No one backs me into a corner or tells me what to do, Sunny. I am in control of my destiny, not the other way around."

"Look, I am not enjoying this, either," Sunny yelled. "But it's interfering with both our professional lives. People are giving me so much sympathy at the factory I can't get any work done. Like it or not, we have to do something to control the damage. Proclaiming our innocence hasn't helped. The only solution is marriage." And wouldn't her parents just faint if they found out she had married a small-town doctor, instead of a big corporate giant. It might be worth it, just to see the stunned looks on their faces. She would no longer have to worry that every eligible male she met had been sent by them.

"Then—" she took a deep breath, determined to make Zach see reason as she continued with her plan "—when we've been together a month or so and people see for themselves that it's not working—and I for one plan to vividly demonstrate that concept for all to see—we'll have our marriage annulled. You can leave and go practice medicine somewhere else—'' Sunny said.

"Not for two years I can't," Zach interrupted. "I have a contract with the state government. They paid my last two years of medical school. In turn, I agreed to practice for two years in whatever rural Tennessee community they could find to cosponsor me.'' That community, of course, had turned out to be Carlisle.

Sunny was aware the town was paying half of Zach's current salary. Her grandfather's company underwrote the living allowance that had bought, among other things, Zach's new truck. And it foot the bill for the day-to-day operating expenses of the clinic. Without Carlisle Furniture Factory, Zach would not have a job. And that made this situation very sticky indeed. Sunny thought it best to keep the information to herself. Apparently he did not know all the specifics behind the monthly check he received from the state.

"So put in for a transfer," Sunny advised. "As soon as you get it, we'll proceed with the annulment. My reputation will be saved. You'll be free and, more importantly, out of Carlisle. No one will ever have to know our marriage was a sham.''

Zach did not want to see Sunny hurt, but he also didn't want to marry. "How's your Land Rover?'' he asked casually to change the subject.

Sunny strode back and forth, her high heels moving soundlessly on the carpeted floor.

Her lips curved ruefully. "I still can't drive it and I've tried darn near everything. I don't think that skunk smell is ever going to go away. But that's my problem, and not something you have to worry about, Zach. Our getting caught in flagrante on my back stoop, however, is a worry we share." Sunny whirled abruptly to face him. She pointed a lecturing finger his way.

"Look, we're young, healthy, vital. No one would believe we could strip down naked in proximity to each other and not even be tempted to kiss."

That wasn't exactly true, Zach thought. He had been tempted. He just hadn't acted.

Her solution made sense. And he had already put in for a transfer out of Carlisle. The problem was, it wouldn't come through for several months, if it came about at all. Meanwhile, he didn't want anyone in Carlisle finding out about it—not even Sunny. "I am going nuts not being able to use my medical training," Zach admitted.

"I'm really tired of this situation interfering with my work over at the furniture factory," Sunny said.

Maybe her solution was worth a shot, Zach thought. "A marriage in name only," he stipulated firmly.

Sunny nodded. "That's the only way I'll have it."

Zach paused. "What happens if we change our minds?"

"We won't," she said quickly, drawing an unsteady breath.

Zach studied her. "If we do... is there a possibility the relationship could become intimate?"

Sunny flushed, beginning to feel as though she were in an "I Love Lucy" episode again. She trembled as he neared her. "Boy, you don't pull any punches, do you?"

"I like to know what my options are. And you didn't answer my question."

Sunny had the feeling a lot was riding on her answer. "Only if it was what we both wanted. But I have to warn you, Zach, the chances of that happening ... are next to nil."

SUNNY WAS FOOLING herself if she believed their marriage was going to be simple and uncomplicated, Zach thought as he dressed for the bachelor party cum poker game. Even if they were married three or four weeks, there were bound to be problems, the least of which was the mutual attraction simmering between them. Sunny might want to pretend it didn't exist, but he saw it every time he looked deep into her whiskey-colored eyes. He hadn't even kissed her yet, and he had an idea how she would taste. Sweet as sugar, hot as fire. Putting them under one roof was not a good idea, but as she'd said, what choice did they have?

When Zach arrived at Slim's grocery store everyone was ready to play poker.

One of the men, George, set out the subs and beer, dill pickles and chips. "Hope you brought your wallet with you, Doc," he teased. "We take our games serious here."

His wallet was not the problem, Zach thought. It was Gramps. Unless Zach was mistaken, he was in obvious discomfort. The glass of bicarb and water in his hand was the first clue. Zach said hello to the rest of the guys and moved over to Augustus Carlisle's side. A fine sheen of perspiration dotted his upper lip. "You're in pain," Zach said in his ear.

"So I am," Gramps admitted, taking another sip of bicarb.

"What'd you do today, Augustus?" George asked, as he pulled the chairs up around the table.

"I moved some files from my office into Sunny's," he replied.

Zach moved around so his back was to the guys. "Where does it hurt?" he asked, very quietly. Augustus looked scared.

"Here." Augustus placed his hand on the center of his chest, then over his heart, toward his left shoulder.

"Any numbness? Tingling?" Zach asked. Augustus shook his head. "I want to run an EKG on you," Zach continued.

"You can't do that now!" Gramps shot back.

"You guys about ready?" a man named Fergus asked, snapping the cards.

Zach turned around and gave the men a sheepish grin. "I left my wallet over at the clinic. Gramps doesn't believe me, so he's going with me to retrieve it." Zach wrapped an arm around Augustus's shoulder. "Back in a minute." He winked at the guys. "Don't start without us."

"YOU SEE, I told you my EKG would be normal," Gramps said, buttoning his shirt, then his fishing vest over that.

Zach folded the readout from the machine and slipped it into a file jacket bearing Augustus's name. He was relieved it was not a heart attack, too. "There's a reason for the pain you were having a few minutes ago," he said. "You need more tests, ones I'm not equipped to do here." Zach wanted to determine the cause, then treat the problem, whatever it was.

To Zach's frustration, Augustus waved off the suggestion. "More tests would be a waste of time and money."

"Sunny wouldn't think so." If Augustus wouldn't do it for himself, maybe he'd do it for his granddaughter.

Augustus's face turned dark. "I forbid you to mention it to her—or anyone else, for that matter. I'm fine. I'm just getting older, that's all. Now, let's get back to the game!"

Zach recognized denial when he saw it. He stopped Augustus at the door. "It's not good to keep secrets. Sunny has a right to know if you're ill."

"Let's get something straight, young man," Augustus lectured, his normal feistiness returning as the last of his mysterious chest pain faded. "I am not going to ruin Sunny's wedding tomorrow with any worries about me. And neither are you! One way or another, you are walking up that aisle to the altar tomorrow to say your 'I do'!"

"Now, SWEETHEART, stop looking so nervous. You're doing the right thing," Gramps soothed Sunny in the anteroom behind the altar in the community church. He was dressed in his best suit and tie, and seeing his contented expression, she couldn't help but think maybe he wasn't so much angry as delighted to see her in this mess. He had wanted a great-grandchild for a long time. Sunny was his only grandchild, and therefore his only hope for one.

"Then why don't I feel more relaxed?" Sunny asked. She didn't know how she'd let her aunt Gertrude and Gertie's friend Matilda talk her into wearing her grandmother's wedding gown, but she had. Standing before the mirror in ivory lace, a veil on her head, she was aware what a hoax she was perpetrating on the people of Carlisle.

"All brides are nervous." Gertie tucked a new blue-and-white hankie in the long sleeve of Sunny's gown. She fastened a borrowed antique locket around her neck. "That's just the way you're supposed to feel."

All brides were not marrying a complete stranger, Sunny thought. Of course, her marriage to Zach was not going to be real. It was only a temporary arrangement. Once it was over, she would use her "broken heart" to fend off any further attempts at matchmaking on her behalf.

The organist began the "Wedding March." "Guess this is it." Gramps took Sunny's elbow and led her around to the back of the church.

Zach was waiting at the altar, beside the minister. He looked resplendent in a dark suit and tie. Gazing up into his face, Sunny could find no visible evidence that he was being forced into this.

He was a better sport than she had figured he would be. Unless, she thought uncomfortably, he planned to get more out of this than she had promised him. Pushing the unwelcome thought aside, she stood next to Zach and faced the minister. Her hands were shaking as she held the bouquet in front of her. All too soon, the minister had finished his introductory remarks about the seriousness of marriage. Sunny was handing her bouquet to Aunt Gertie and turning to face Zach.

"Do you, Sunny, promise to love, honor and cherish Zach for as long as you both shall live?"

As long as it lasts, she amended silently. "I do," Sunny said. She looked deep into Zach's eyes. He looked into hers. A thrill went through her. She knew they were only doing this for everyone else, but dressed in wedding clothes and standing before a church full of people, she found it hard to remember that this was all just pretend.

"Do you, Zach, promise to love, honor and cherish Sunny for as long as you both shall live?"

Zach took her hand in his, held it warmly. As he gazed at her his eyes glinted with a subdued humor, as if he could hardly believe he was going through with this, too. "I do."

Under the minister's direction, Sunny and Zach exchanged rings. The minister grinned at Zach. "You may kiss the bride, son."

Sunny's breath stalled in her lungs as Zach took her masterfully into his arms. He lowered his mouth to hers. Electricity sizzled through Sunny at the brief, but sensual, contact.

Appearing quite pleased with himself, Zach stepped back. The organist resumed playing. To Sunny's relief—or was it disappointment?—it was over.

"I DIDN'T KNOW it was possible for anyone to blush for three hours straight," Zach remarked in Sunny's ear after he swept her up into his arms and carried her across the threshold, into her home.

Arms still hooked around his neck, Sunny gave him an adoring look that, she assured herself, was strictly for the benefit of the crowd of onlookers who had accompanied them on the short walk from the church to her home. Smiling up at him, she whispered, "When I agreed to marry you, I didn't know a wedding was included." Then, turning to those still watching them, she lifted her hand in a merry wave. The crowd waved back.

Zach gently set her down and wrapped an arm around her waist. Tugging her close, he leaned down and whispered in her ear, "Seems like everyone in town is rooting for us." Zach glanced at Augustus in the crowd. Sunny's grandfather seemed fine this morning, but Zach was still worried. He'd have to do his best to keep an eye on Gramps from afar until he could get him into the hospital for a complete series of tests.

Sunny allowed herself to lean into Zach's side only because she was tired from all the festivities. "They want you to do right by me," she admitted. With one last wave at the crowd, they stepped back, inside the foyer, and shut the door.

Exhausted, she leaned against it. Zach propped a hand next to her head and looked down at her. For one insane second, she thought he was going to kiss her again, really kiss her. A sizzle of desire swept through her.

Zach's gaze swept her upturned face in leisurely fashion. "That's quite an old-fashioned notion, even for southern and proper Tennessee, don't you think?"

"Quite. But that's the town of Carlisle for you," Sunny said lightly. "In fact, the sense of family, community, caring and warmth is one of the things I like best about the town.''

"You don't find the intrusion of others into our private life annoying?" Zach asked. He did.

Sunny apparently knew what he was referring to. "I sidestepped the invitation for the honeymoon cabin, didn't I?"

"Yes, although I don't think anyone was pleased about it.''

"We can't help it. We both have to work," Sunny said stubbornly. She folded her arms in front of her, still radiantly beautiful in her veil and wedding dress.

"I don't tonight," Zach said, "unless someone gets sick."

"Well, unfortunately, I do have to work. All the brouhaha of late has left me behind."

Zach was surprised at his own unwillingness to have the festivities end. "You're not going into the office!" He had an idea what chaos an action like that would cause.

"No, of course not, silly," Sunny said, slipping off her veil. "I brought all the work home with me."

Zach didn't find that much more reassuring. "Don't you think we should get to know each other a little better if we're going to be sharing space?"

"Eventually," Sunny said with a cool smile that arrowed straight to his heart. "Not tonight." She slipped from beneath his outstretched arm. "I made up the guest room for you. Shall I show you where you'll be bunking?"

Zach nodded. He moved his arm in gallant fashion. "After you."

Zach followed her up the stairs. They creaked beneath her weight, and a little more beneath his. At the top of the stairs was the master bedroom. A large brass bed dominated the room. It was covered with a patchwork quilt and numerous pillows. Sunny moved on down the hall, past the linen closet and the bath. "We're going to have to share the bathroom while you're here," she informed him with a sigh. "This is an old house, and there's only the one."

"I think I can rough it," Zach said. But that was before he'd seen his bed.

SUNNY SPENT her wedding night in a buttercup yellow sweatsuit and white cotton socks. She curled up on her bed, writing and rewriting letters on behalf of Carlisle Furniture, soliciting more business for the company on her laptop computer. She could hear Zach roaming around downstairs. She felt a little guilty for sticking him in the tiny guest room, where the rollaway bed was half the size needed to accommodate his tall, rangy frame, but that couldn't be helped on such short notice. Besides, she reassured herself, he wouldn't be here long.

Around 10:00 p.m., Zach knocked. Sunny kept typing. "Come in," she said, without looking up from her keyboard.

Zach carried a tray in. It had a pot of tea, a sandwich and some wedding cake. "I could hear you typing. I thought you might like something to eat," he said.

"Thanks for the tray. I'm sorry if I disturbed you." A tingle of awareness rushing through her, Sunny kept typing.

Zach lingered in the doorway. "What are you working on?"

"Business letters."

"Oh."

For a second, Zach appeared so lonely Sunny's heart went out to him. She thought about how it must be for him. Newly married to a woman he didn't even know. And Carlisle wasn't exactly a hot spot. TV reception was spotty at best, and cable was not available. A few people in town had satellite dishes. Sunny wasn't one of them.

"Can I do anything to help? Address envelopes or something?"

Sunny shook her head.

"Can I get you something else to eat or drink?"

He wants company. Sunny had grown up feeling the loneliest child in the world. Seeing it in Zach made her heart ache. Finished with the letter she was working on, she put her laptop aside. "This is fine. Did you get something for yourself?"

Zach nodded. "I also did a hundred sit-ups and push-ups, put all my clothes away and read the last four issues of the *Journal of the American Medical Association.*"

"Bored out of your mind, right?"

Zach nodded. "How do you stand it here?"

"I've got plenty to keep me busy."

"That isn't what I meant."

"I know, but I'm not interested in discussing my romantic life prior to you." It was just too embarrassing. Besides, she didn't want Zach to know how she'd been duped.

"Too late," he said smugly. "There were some hints dropped at the bachelor party last night."

Sunny froze. "Exactly what did you hear?" She was going to kill those men!

"That you were engaged to one Andrew Singleton III shortly after arriving in Carlisle to take over your grandfather's company."

Sunny felt the blood rush to her face. "Yes, well, that was a mistake."

"No one really knows what happened to break the two of you up," Zach continued.

And no one was going to know, not if she had anything to do about it, Sunny thought stubbornly. She forced a smile. "We weren't suited to each other, all right?"

"Still carrying a torch for him?"

"Heavens, no!"

Zach raised a brow skeptically, seeming to know there was much she wasn't saying. Even more disturbing was the awareness that he wouldn't rest until he did know it all.

"If you don't mind, I'd like to change the subject," Sunny said prudently.

"No problem." Zach grinned. "So how's the factory doing?"

"Okay. It could be better, though. That's why I'm writing letters to solicit new business. In the past, the company has only sold furniture to other independently owned stores in the state. I think we could do a lot better if we expanded our markets."

"Hence the letters." He nodded at the stack of neatly typed envelopes beside her.

Sunny nodded. "That's not the only change I'm making, however. I've arranged for a computer-run order-entry system that will be on-line twenty-four hours a day, and I'm also putting together a catalog of mail-order items."

"That is a lot."

"Which is why I'm so busy." Sunny took the time to show him glossy color photos of their new rustically designed Tennessee Cabin line of furniture. "I've even been thinking of purchasing a few pieces at employee discount for my house. You may have noticed my guest room needs a little work."

"I noticed."

Zach leaned against the bureau, radiating all the pure male power and casual sexiness of a big screen hero. Unbidden, all sorts of romantic thoughts and fantasies came to mind. Sunny pushed them away.

She finished her sandwich and tea. "Well, thanks for the supper, but I've got to get back to work now."

Zach moved toward her gallantly. "Let me get that for you."

Sunny caught a whiff of his brisk, sexy scent and backed away. She hoped he had no idea how much having him in her bedroom this way was affecting her. "I can handle it."

"No. Really. Let me."

"Zach," Sunny insisted, as heat began to center in her chest, then moved outward in radiating waves, "you don't have to wait on me."

They both tugged at once . . . and let go. The tray went crashing to the floor. And so did Sunny's china. She grabbed a wastebasket and knelt to pick up the pieces. Zach knelt beside her.

"I'm sorry," he said.

"It's okay," Sunny said, unable to keep the irritation completely from her voice. Having him in such proximity seemed to make her all thumbs. Unless she got ahold of herself, who knew what else might happen?

"Where do you keep your vacuum cleaner?" he asked.

"In the hall closet downstairs."

He retrieved it. While he started sweeping the immediate area, in an effort to pick up all remaining tiny shards of glass, Sunny carried the wastebasket of broken dishes out to the trash. As she was carefully transferring the contents, the neighbor's dog ran into her yard, barking.

Matilda followed. Quickly she took in Sunny's jogging suit, sweat socks and bunny slippers. "Sunny, for heaven's sake! What are you doing taking out the trash on your wedding night?"

Sunny felt herself turning red as she offered an airy wave. "Oh, we broke some dishes. Nothing to worry about."

Briefly Matilda looked worried. Composing herself hurriedly, she advised, "Well, have fun, darlin'. Einstein, come here! We have to finish our evening walk!"

Sunny walked back inside. She carried the wastebasket back to her bedroom.

Zach straightened as she tried to sidle past him unnoticed and caught hold of her. The next thing she knew, she was anchored against him, hip to breast. He was grinning down at her, evidently enjoying the perfect way their bodies meshed, and in no hurry at all to let her go.

"Nervous, aren't you?" he said softly.

"I don't—"

"It's okay. I am, too. And I know why. Sometimes in medicine the cure is worse than the disease. And sometimes in romance the anticipation of a situation is more unnerving than the actual event. So maybe we should just get this over with," he said, and then his mouth came down to cover hers.

Caught off guard, she felt her mouth soften beneath his. Not again, she thought, alarmed. But even as her mind was telling her no, her body was already saying yes....

The kiss in the church had been properly restrained. This kiss was claiming her as his woman, Sunny noted, as Zach began a deep, achingly sweet exploration of her mouth.

And claim her he did, his mouth moving possessively over hers, his tongue coaxing her lips apart, drawing her deeper and deeper into the sensual battle, until she was no longer sure of anything but his strong arms and body, and the wonder of his mouth, and his sizzling, yet tender kiss.

Excitement pouring through her, Sunny wreathed her arms about Zach's neck. Surrendering to his will, she surged against him and felt her knees turn to butter. Murmuring his encouragement, he gathered her closer, enveloping her masterfully in his warmth and strength. He kissed her again, long and deeply, the hunger inside him matching hers. And though it warmed her, it left her feeling hollow, too. Wanting more…needing…Sunny thought dizzily—she wasn't quite sure what.

Reveling in the sheer intensity and wonder of their embrace, she sighed her pleasure softly. Zach's hand slid down her back, guiding her nearer. Sunny's breasts were crushed against the hardness of his chest. Lower still, she felt the unmistakable proof of his desire, the rock-hard brace of his thighs. With a start, she realized where things were headed if she didn't halt this forward pass of his right now.

It didn't matter how accomplished a lover Zach Grainger was. She had no intention of making this a real honeymoon.

Hand to his chest, she broke off the sizzling embrace. "What was that for?" she gasped.

"Because you look so good in those yellow sweats," he murmured, ducking his head once again.

Sunny sucked in another quick breath and wrested herself from his embrace. Heart pounding, she smoothed her tousled hair from her face. "You can't…I never said I'd—damn it, Zach, what do you think you're doing?"

He gently traced her cheekbone with his thumb, then bent to kiss her temple. "I'm making life more interesting."

"I don't want my life to be more interesting," Sunny insisted.

"That's not what your lips said when you were kissing me just now," he teased, his clear blue eyes glinting with humor. "It's not what your lips said when you kissed me back after the ceremony."

"That was all for show," Sunny huffed.

"Keep putting on a show like that and no one will believe our claims of annulment later on." Arms folded in front of him, he leaned close, his eyes twinkling. "And besides, if you didn't want me to notice you, how come you're wearing a different perfume tonight than you were this afternoon?"

"I'm notoriously absentminded when I have a lot of work to do," Sunny fibbed.

"Funny," Zach drawled, giving her the slow, sensual once-over. "You strike me as a woman who'd be in perfect control of her faculties all the time."

That had been true, Sunny thought. Until Zach had charged into her life. "Well, I am. Absentminded. Sometimes. I mean."

"Hmm." He rubbed his jaw contemplatively. "I guess I'll have to take your word for that."

"Not to worry, Zach," Sunny assured him, feeling yet again as if she were in an "I Love Lucy" episode. "It won't happen anymore!"

His expression was one of comically exaggerated misunderstanding. "No more perfume?" he asked sadly.

Sunny flushed, aware he had gotten under her skin in a way no man ever had. "No more anything!" she said firmly.

"Now, Sunny," he teased, his gaze sliding over her, "don't make any promises you can't keep. Especially since we have the rest of our honeymoon weekend ahead of us."

Sunny tossed her hair. "I've never made any promises I couldn't keep," she vowed hotly. "Furthermore, you're the one who is in for a surprise! Now, out!" Her pulse pounding as she half anticipated another kiss, she pushed him out of her bedroom and slammed the door.

From the other side of the door, Zach chuckled softly, victoriously, then sauntered away. Sunny waited for his footsteps to recede all the way down the hall, then let go of the breath she had been holding. Her knees were so weak and trembly she nearly collapsed against the door. Leaning against it, she knotted her damp hands in front of her and briefly closed her eyes.

Zach could call this whatever he liked, but now that she'd had a moment to contemplate it, she knew darn well what this newfound behavior of his was all about. It wasn't so much desire as his payback to her for having been forced by her family and friends into marrying her. Obviously he blamed her for their predicament. Hence, he intended to extract his own style of vengeance by torturing her with kisses and treating her like a real wife and potential lover every chance he got.

Well, Sunny surmised grimly, her usual confidence returning, Zach was fooling himself if he thought he was going to get the best of her. She could torture him, too...simply by turning herself into the kind of wife he *wouldn't* want.

Chapter Three

Take Me as I Am

If he didn't know better, Zach thought, as he awoke to the delicious smells of blueberry muffins and hot coffee, he'd think he'd fallen into a velvet-lined trap. Here he was, in Carlisle less than three weeks, and he had a beautiful wife who even cooked him breakfast.

Not that he had ever expected to find himself in this position. He had figured that the scandal would die down if he just imposed an iron will and stayed away from her. And, Zach admitted honestly, it had taken all his strength to stay clear of the local angel with the red-gold hair.

But the uproar over Sunny's compromising hadn't died down. And that was her fault, too. After all, he might have been a virtual newcomer, but she resided in town. She should never have stripped down out there in the country or induced him to do the same no matter how skunky their clothes had been. She should have known the odds were they'd get caught sneaking back into town. Particularly since her grandfather had worried when she hadn't shown up for dinner and had been out looking for her.

Which brought him to the marriage. He had agreed to it, but that didn't mean he'd had to like it. He hated losing control of his life. But he had tried to make the best of this mutually bad situation they found themselves in by taking the supper to her the evening before. He hadn't anticipated kissing her; that had just happened. And though he had no plans of staying in Carlisle, he did want to make love to her. And if their lovemaking was even one-tenth as sweet as their kisses had been, well, who knew what would happen after that? Zach mused happily as he rolled out of bed and grabbed a robe.

Her fixing breakfast for them *had* to be a good sign. It meant she was willing to meet him halfway on this. Zach's smile faded as soon as he walked into the kitchen.

Sunny sat at the kitchen table. Her gorgeous hair was wrapped in curlers. She had something that looked like whipped cream smeared all over her face. She was wearing an oversize man's shirt that was stained with paint. Her jeans were old and ripped at the knees. The kitchen was a huge mess. The muffin tin stood empty.

Trying hard not to laugh—for Sunny could not be anything but beautiful to him, no matter how she outfitted herself—Zach strolled over to pour himself some coffee. He wasn't surprised to find the carafe was bone-dry.

"There aren't any more muffins," she said.

Zach's glance roved her slender figure in a sensual way designed to annoy her. "You ate a dozen muffins all by yourself?" he asked mildly.

"I only made two." Wielding a pair of scissors, she continued cutting out big patches of the morning paper.

Zach noted with chagrin she had done particular damage to the sports page. He could get another newspaper. He could also easily make another pot of coffee. The muffins were another matter. "I didn't know you could make just two muffins," he said casually.

"I cut the recipe down to size."

If she could do it, he could, too. He began to look around for a recipe and ingredients.

"I also used up the last of the blueberries." She hid her grin behind her full coffee cup.

Zach knew she was giving him hell. Whether it was to punish him for kissing her the night before or discourage him from doing it again didn't really matter. He could handle her. In fact, as she would soon find out, he could dish it out, as well. Sunny, the darling princess of Carlisle, might be used to having her own way all the time, but that was going to change.

"I think I'll go back upstairs and get dressed," Zach announced laconically.

"You do that," Sunny murmured in an unconcerned voice as she buried her nose in the morning paper.

"You just wait, honey," he whispered, a smile of anticipation on his lips. "I'll best you yet."

SUNNY WANTED to leave the face mask on all day, just to irritate Zack, but she was afraid of what would happen to her skin, so she rinsed it off in the kitchen sink and replaced it with a thick coating of winter-strength moisturizer. Satisfied her face had a disgusting oily gleam to it that would be bound to discourage any further kisses from her new husband, she went back to cutting more holes in the morning paper.

Seconds later, loud footsteps sounded on the stairs. Zach walked into the kitchen. Sunny never would have believed it, but the rascal had outdone her.

He was dressed in a white undershirt that was ripped down the center, white socks, black shoes and high-water pants. She wasn't sure what he had put on his hair, but he had fixed it with numerous cowlicks spiked up in the back. He hadn't shaved and the morning beard gave him a piratical look.

Zach cleared a place on the counter with a swipe of his arm that sent even more flour flying. ''Think I'll fix me a little breakfast,'' he said.

Taking that to be her cue to leave, Sunny slipped out of the kitchen and back up the stairs. Now what? she wondered as she barricaded herself in her bedroom. She had wanted him to know this marriage, temporary or not, was going to be no picnic with free sex. She hadn't counted on him trying to outdo her.

If she backed off now—by acting and dressing normally—he would think he had won. Therefore, Sunny decided, she would just have to tough out the rest of the weekend. She only had twenty hours and forty-three minutes left before she could go to work again.

The rest of the morning passed quickly. She had a few bad moments when she smelled the hash brown potatoes cooking. That was, after all, her favorite dish. But she forced herself to stay in her bedroom and get some more Carlisle-company work done. It was the sound of the baseball game on the radio that eventually drew her out. It was loud enough to be heard in every room of the house, and worse, it was a doubleheader, which meant it would be on for hours.

Wanting something to eat, she ambled on back downstairs.

Squelching the urge to ask him to turn the radio down, she headed for the kitchen. It was in an even bigger mess than she had left it. Zach walked in behind her. His closeness made her senses spin.

"Where do you keep your spittoon?" he asked in an innocent voice.

Hanging on to her temper with effort, Sunny whirled to face him. Like her, he had done nothing to improve his appearance. They looked like characters in a comedy show.

Ignoring the sudden heavy jump in her pulse, she smiled at him firmly. "I don't have a spittoon," she replied calmly.

Zach slowly ripped open a pouch of chewing tobacco. "Then where am I going to put my spit?"

Sunny had put up with a lot, but there were limits, even if she had to sacrifice a little pride to enforce them. "You are not doing that in my house," she announced firmly.

"It's our house now, sugar," he corrected, patting her rollers condescendingly with the flat of his hand. "And don't worry about not having a spittoon for me right off the bat. I forgive you."

"You are so—" As Sunny sputtered for words that would be precise yet ladylike, Zach edged closer. As he neared her, the room seemed to do a half spin.

"What?" Zach's eyes took on a predatory gleam.

"Thoughtful," Sunny said.

"Aren't I?" He turned away from her and opened the cupboard. "I suppose I could put a teacup in every room and use that in lieu of a spittoon."

Sunny slipped between Zach and her teacups and crossed her arms in front of her. "Over my dead body."

"Is that a challenge?"

Sunny's temper began to flame. "Babe," she drawled, "it's an ultimatum."

Zach grinned at her and plucked a big wad of tobacco from the pouch. "Don't you dare," she said. "Zach, I swear—"

He kept going anyway. She grabbed for the pouch with one hand and knocked the pinch from his fingers with the other. Loose tobacco sprayed the floor at the exact moment he stepped forward, trapping her against the counter. "Give me my tobacco back," he ordered mildly, one hand braced on either side of her.

Sunny's heart pounded at his proximity. Even in the outrageous getup he was enormously attractive. But she was *not* giving in. "If you want to do something that disgusting, you can do it outside," she said, clutching the pouch and trying not to think about the intimate way his muscled thighs were now pressing against hers.

Zach's dimples deepened. "What if I want to do something even more disgusting inside?" he whispered.

The way he dipped his head toward her mouth caused a distinct melting sensation in her knees.

Oh, no. He was going to kiss her again. Sunny sucked in a breath, determined not to let him make her feel all weak and hot and compliant again, and turned her head to the side. Her eyes widened as she saw Aunt Gertie, Matilda and a very pregnant Rhonda-Faye Pearson on the other side of the screen door. Sunny exchanged mortified glances with Rhonda-Faye, knowing that if anyone could understand even an inkling of what was going on here, it would be her best friend. And even that, Sunny thought, studying Rhonda-Faye's stunned expression, would be a stretch.

"Oh, dear," Gertie said, shifting the foil-wrapped casserole dish in her hand.

The sole proprietor of the town's only department store, Gertie felt it her duty to dress with perfect panache and style all the time. Her polished appearance only made Sunny feel all the more comically disheveled.

"It appears we've come at an inopportune time," Gertie said.

The forty-five-year-old Matilda was not only Sunny's friend and nearest neighbor, but also a key employee over at the furniture factory. "We rang the bell, dear," she said, putting a plump hand to her cheek.

"I guess you all didn't hear since the radio was on so loud," Rhonda-Faye added, looking resplendent in a white maternity outfit.

"So we came around to the back," Gertie continued, flattening one white-gloved hand over the signature pearl necklace around her neck. "We brought you some dinner so you wouldn't have to cook while you were on your honeymoon. But I can see that you two already have been cooking."

Sunny was so embarrassed she wanted to sink right through the floor. She never had a messy kitchen!

And as for their appearances, she recollected in silent misery, this was going to be all over town in no time.

"Thank you so much. Zach and I were just goofing around, weren't we, honey?" Sunny elbowed him in the ribs.

"It's been a barrel of laughs so far," he said.

Sunny turned to Zach and gave him a glare only he could see. *Help me out here,* she ordered with her eyes.

"Well, we'll be going, dear. If you're sure that everything is okay?" Gertie said, taking in their mutually comical state.

Rhonda-Faye giggled and backed out the door. "I think we ought to leave, ladies, and let these two get back to whatever it was they were doing."

"Thanks for the food. If Sunny doesn't eat it all herself, I'll be in seventh heaven," Zach said.

Sunny gave him another elbow as the ladies laughed. When they were alone again, she faced Zach. Unlike him, she wasn't laughing. "We are in so deep now," she moaned miserably. "You have no idea."

ZACH OPENED the clinic at 9:00 a.m. Monday. Sunny's grandfather marched in at 9:02. Zach eyed her protector with courtesy and respect, hoping this was a professional visit. "What can I do for you, Mr. Carlisle?" he asked politely.

"You can call me 'Augustus', now that we're related," he said, fastening his piercing eyes on Zach. "And there's nothing wrong with me—today anyway—so you can put that darn stethoscope away. I just came in to talk."

Zach had been afraid of that. "About what?"

"Sunny, what else. I heard what went on over at your home yesterday."

Zach had had a feeling it would get all over town. He had not expected to have to endure any lectures on his behavior.

"If you sincerely want to make a go of your marriage to my granddaughter, son, you are going to have to work a little harder."

Had the marriage to Sunny been a real one, Zach would have worked hard.

"You do want to make a go of this marriage, don't you?" Augustus persisted.

It was funny. The day he had agreed to marry Sunny, making a go of the ill-advised union had been the last thing on his mind. Seeing her in a wedding dress, holding her in his arms, kissing her, had softened his resistance somewhat. To his surprise, her orneriness had appealed to him even more. Zach liked the idea of a little mischief in his wife.

"Of course I want what's best for Sunny," Zach said honestly, aware Augustus was still waiting for an answer.

"Yes, well, Sunny is more fragile than she appears," Augustus warned.

"She seems inordinately strong willed to me," Zach disagreed.

"About business, yes. But her personal life hasn't always been easy."

"Are you taking about her broken engagement again?" he asked.

Augustus frowned and held up a warning hand. "I've said too much as it is. If Sunny wants you to know about her life before she came to Carlisle, she'll tell you. In the meantime, if you plan to stay married to my granddaughter, you need to shave, even on weekends."

"Yes, sir."

Augustus looked Zach up and down. "You be good to my granddaughter, you hear? I expect you to treat her with the love and respect she deserves."

Again Zach nodded. He didn't mind the lecture nearly as much as he expected. Maybe because he saw the love Augustus felt for Sunny. As for the marriage, he knew he should have minded that more than he did, even if it was only a temporary social fix for a local scandal. He needed to be careful not to get too involved here. He had his own life to live.

"SUNNY, I AM SORRY, but I will never get the hang of this new computer," Matilda said late Monday afternoon.

"Yes, you will. Just give it time."

"I have. But I just can't remember anything that Chuck Conway told me to do," Matilda said with a sigh.

"Then maybe he needs to come back and show you how to work this new order-entry system again," Sunny said. "I'll call him right now and set up a time."

No sooner was Sunny off the phone than Aunt Gertie appeared in the doorway to Sunny's office. "May I have a word with you, sugarplum?"

"Sure." Sunny knew it had to be important. Otherwise Gertie never would have left Carlisle Department Store during business hours.

She came in, shut the door behind her and inched off her gloves. "Sugarplum, I am gonna be frank with you. I don't know what your mama and daddy told you about marriage—"

"Gertie, this isn't a sex talk, is it?"

"Well. Sort of. I mean I—I expect you know about the birds and bees."

"Yes, ma'am, I do."

"But there's a lot more to sex and marriage than just the birds and the bees," Gertie continued seriously.

Sunny tried, but could not contain a flush of embarrassment. "Aunt Gertie, I love you for trying to help me out on this, but we couldn't save this talk for another time?"

Gertie patted Sunny's shoulder fondly. "Sugarplum, after what I saw at your home yesterday morning, I think we need to have this talk now, before any more damage is done to this sweet new union of yours."

Sunny could see there was going to be no getting out of this lecture. When Aunt Gertie had something on her mind, she did not rest until she had said it. Sunny sat down. Gertie took her hand in hers.

"First of all, technically speaking, you are still on your honeymoon. And it's important for you to act like a newlywed. And not wear curlers in your hair and goo on your face and old clothes. Even on weekend mornings.''

Her embarrassment fading, Sunny folded her arms in front of her. ''I'm not going to pretend to be something I'm not,'' she told her aunt stubbornly.

''Good. Because you're not the kind of woman who goes around with curlers in your hair. Unless, of course, you're trying to send that new husband of yours a message that you aren't interested in him sexually.''

''Aunt Gertie!'' Her face flaming, Sunny bolted up off the sofa.

Gertie patted her own perfect bob of red-gold curls. ''We may as well speak frankly, sugarplum. I know this marriage of yours was more or less arranged.''

''Against my will and better judgment, I might add,'' Sunny interjected, as she paced back and forth.

''But that young man of yours is quite a catch. He's a doctor, he's kind and good-looking and your age and he's from Tennessee.''

''But he's not going to stay in Carlisle,'' Sunny said, deciding now was as good a time as any to lay the groundwork for her and Zach's eventual annulment. Sunny planted her feet firmly on the carpet and regarded her great-aunt willfully. ''I am.''

''He'll be here for two years. Who knows what can happen in that time? You might have a baby. He might change his mind about leaving.''

''It's still an arranged marriage,'' Sunny persisted, trying not to let herself get sidetracked with idyllic images of Zach and a baby.

''Oh, I know arranged marriages aren't really an 'in' thing these days, but they do work. My own marriage to your uncle Fergus was arranged, and we've been married for nearly forty years now."

"I know, and I'm glad you're happy, but—"

A knock sounded on the door. Matilda poked her head in. She was beaming. Sunny frowned, instantly knowing from the excitement crackling in the air that something was up.

"We're ready," Matilda sang out.

A group of women burst through the doors to Sunny's office. They were all carrying gaily wrapped gifts. Matilda came last, wheeling in a pink-and-white cake in the shape of a wedding bell and a crystal bowl of pink-lemonade punch.

"Surprise!" everyone shouted.

"We're giving you a wedding shower," Rhonda-Faye said.

"Rhonda-Faye made the cake over at the diner."

Sunny smiled at her friends. This was what she liked about living in Carlisle. The closeness and camaraderie. The way everyone watched out for everyone else. She had never had that growing up and she had missed it dearly.

"This is wonderful! Thank you!" She hugged everyone in turn and then settled in to enjoy the party.

It was only after the gifts had been opened, the games played and the cake eaten that Gertie stood to make an announcement. "We have one last present for you, Sunny."

"I can't imagine what," Sunny joked. "You've already given me everything but the kitchen sink. Cookbooks, nightgowns, several bottles of blackberry wine."

"But this is something really special," Gertie said.

"Yes," Matilda added. "We all know how you love to learn, Sunny."

"So we pitched in and hired an instructor for you," Gertie said.

"An instructor on what?" Sunny asked, visions of Masters and Johnson textbooks dancing in her head.

"On how to be happily married, of course," Gertie explained.

Matilda leaned forward excitedly. "The course tells you everything you need to know about being a good, loving wife in five easy lessons that are spaced out over a period of two weeks."

Oh, my gosh. "This is so sweet, really—" Sunny began.

"Honey, you don't have to be embarrassed," Aunt Gertie soothed. "We know the newlywed phase isn't easy."

The very pregnant Rhonda-Faye nodded. "We've all been there. And we all feel we have something to learn, too." She leaned forward earnestly. "I mean, what marriage couldn't be made better?"

"What are you saying?" Sunny asked with trepidation.

"We all signed up to take the course with you," Rhonda-Faye replied, her excitement about the endeavor evident.

"So what do you say?" Matilda asked enthusiastically. "Are you ready for your first lesson?"

Chapter Four

That Kind of Girl

"Getting pretty busy here, aren't you, Doc," Fergus Walker said when he came in to have his blood pressure checked the next day.

That was a matter of opinion. Zach wasn't doing nearly as much for the community as he could, given half a chance. "I've seen four patients here today," Zach said dryly, noting it was nearly 6:00 p.m., closing time for the clinic. "I think I'm setting a record."

"Now, now, don't you fret none," Fergus said as he pushed up the light blue sleeve of his post-office uniform. Fergus watched as Zach fitted the blood-pressure cuff around his upper arm. "As word filters out around the mountain that you done right by Sunny, folks will be lining up to see you, 'cause it's either that or a sixty-mile trip to the nearest doctor."

"Sixty-five," Zach corrected absently, already pumping air into the cuff.

Fergus was silent as Zach read his blood pressure. "So how am I doing, Doc?"

Not as good as he would have liked, considering Sunny's uncle was only fifty-five. "How long have you been on your current medication?" Zach asked, pulling the stethoscope from his ears.

Fergus stroked the handlebars of his thick black mustache. "About two years now, I reckon."

"And the dosage is—?"

Fergus told him. "Why do you ask?"

Zach went to the cupboard and pulled out a sample packet of pills. "Your blood pressure is a little high. I think you might do better on this."

Fergus shrugged uninterestedly. "Whatever you think, Doc, will be fine. Now, back to that new bride of yours—"

"I wasn't aware we were discussing Sunny," Zach said, already writing out a prescription.

Fergus stroked the ends of his mustache. "C'mon, Doc, don't mess with me. I know what happened over the weekend. Hell, everybody in town knows."

"Well, that makes me feel better," Zach drawled. Not that he was surprised about this. Fergus was married to Gertie—one of the eyewitnesses.

Fergus stabbed a finger at Zach. "And I know you're probably wondering what you've done, marrying a beautiful gal like that. But I am here to reassure you that damn near anyone can be a good husband. All it takes is a little work."

Zach ripped the prescription off his pad and handed it to Fergus. "Is that so?" he asked blandly.

He knew he should have minded this advice from Fergus more than he did, even if his marriage to Sunny was only temporary. And that puzzled Zach, too.

Sunny Carlisle was still a virtual stranger to him. Why should he have cared whether she was happy or not?

"Yes, sirree. Nevertheless, you're going to have to work a little harder if you want to make a go of this marriage. You do want to, don't you, Doc?"

Zach wouldn't mind making love with Sunny, but as for the rest . . . the idea of being married to anyone at this point made him feel as though he were suffocating. "To tell you the truth, Mr.—"

"Call me 'Fergus.'"

"I'm not all that sure I'm the marrying kind," Zach confessed.

Fergus's affable grin widened. He clapped Zach on the shoulder. "Then it's high time we changed all that. Now, do you want to do something that will make Sunny sweet on you? 'Cause, if so, I've got just the thing."

ZACH WAS STILL mulling over Fergus's suggestion as he locked up the clinic and drove home. Fergus had had a good idea, although a little corny, but Zach didn't know if he wanted to follow through on it. He didn't really need to get more involved with Sunny than he already was, or make their relationship any more intimate or romantic. Besides, Zach mused as he parked his truck in front of her house, got out and started up the walk, did he want her to think he was the kind of guy who could be pushed, coerced and generally led around by the nose?

Zach heard the temperamental banging of kitchen-cupboard doors from halfway up the walk. He found Sunny in the kitchen, scowling as she slid a plate of food into the microwave. "What's got you in a lather?" he asked.

"I don't want to talk about it!"

But she needed to, he thought. When no other information was forthcoming, he shrugged. "Fine. I'll just call the town grapevine and ask for details there." He pivoted toward the phone on the wall, knowing just about anyone would do, since everyone knew everyone else's business in Carlisle.

Sunny caught up with him as he lifted the receiver from the cradle. Her hand tightened on his wrist, forcing the phone back down.

"Don't."

Zach sucked in a silent breath and tolerated the sizzling warmth of her touch. "Then start speaking," he said gruffly.

Sunny's lower lip pushed out petulantly as she dropped first her gaze, then her hand. "I suppose you'll hear about it anyway."

Briefly she told him about the belated bridal shower the ladies had held for her and their mutual gift. Zach tried to hold in his amusement, but the look of righteous indignation on her face sent him over the edge. He laughed until tears streamed from his eyes and he was doubled over at the waist.

"You, in a class on how to be a loving wife?"

"It's not funny! I am not looking forward to this."

"Oh, but I am," he teased.

"Don't think I am going to turn into some mousy little thing who lives and breathes to do your bidding," Sunny warned.

Zach clapped his palm to his chest in a parody of hopefulness. "I can dream, can't I?"

Sunny removed his hand from his chest and forced it back down to his side. "I'm serious, Zach," she stormed. "I am not looking forward to this."

He appreciated the rosy color in her cheeks and the indignant sparkle in her whiskey-colored eyes more than he knew he should. "So don't go through with it," he advised. "Tell them thanks, but no thanks."

Sunny paced away from him, her hips swaying sexily beneath her trim black skirt.

"I can't do that, either."

"Why not?"

Sunny whirled to face him in a drift of flowery perfume. She pushed the red-gold curls from her face with the heel of her hand.

"Because I'd hurt their feelings. They put a lot of thought into that gift."

"The wrong kind of thought." Zach got a plate out and dipped a generous heap of Gertie's mostaccioli casserole on it. "You're setting a dangerous precedent, allowing them to meddle in our lives this way. Furthermore, I don't know how you tolerate the intrusive behavior of our neighbors."

Sunny watched as he added tossed green salad to a bowl, then Italian dressing. "If you are referring to the other morning, you're lucky it wasn't Gramps who walked in on us."

Zach shrugged. Deciding Sunny needed a salad to round out her meal, he dipped some for her, too. "We have a right to behave any way we want in our own home."

"My home," Sunny corrected, taking the salad he handed her. She carried it to the table. "And maybe we do... but they also had a point. If you and I are going to stay married, even for a little while, we need to do better, Zach. The other morning we both behaved ridiculously.''

"Oh, I don't know.'' Unable to resist teasing her just a little, he sauntered nearer and gave her the once-over. "I kind of like dressing up—or down, as the case may be—every once in a while.''

Sunny's chin set stubbornly as she added a pitcher of freshly brewed iced tea to the center of the table. "Well, I don't like being embarrassed.'' She waved her arms at him, agitatedly punctuating each and every word she spoke. "And I felt like a fool, being caught in that getup, with my kitchen a mess.''

Zach shook his head at her and gave her a censuring glance. "You care too much about what the neighbors think.''

"And you don't care enough.''

Her words were casually—maybe even gently— spoken, but they hit a nerve. It bothered him, too, but he was not able to change the way he felt. Right now he wanted a wall around his heart. Which was yet another reason he never should have let himself be talked into this temporary marriage.

Silence fell between them as Sunny removed her dinner from the microwave and carried her plate to the table. Zach popped his dinner in and pushed buttons. As he waited for it to heat, he regarded her curiously, realizing she was as much a mystery to him as he was to her. "Why doesn't all this bother you?''

Sunny sat down at the table, spread her napkin on her lap, then waited for him to join her. "Maybe because I know what it's like to have the shoe on the other foot.''

Zach stared at her. "You mean you were ostracized for something else?"

"No, silly," she said as the microwave buzzer sounded. "I mean I didn't always live here."

Zach carried his plate over and joined her at the table. "Where did you live?"

"Various European countries. My parents are both international-law attorneys. They specialize in helping U.S. companies expand their operations overseas and are generally involved in the setup and so on. It's difficult, demanding work."

"So you moved around a lot as a kid."

"At least once a year. Sometimes more."

"That sounds exciting."

Sunny stared down at her half-eaten casserole. "I suppose it had its advantages," she said carefully.

Zach read between the lines. "But you didn't see what those advantages were at the time, did you?" he said softly.

Again she was silent. Zach could tell he was probing too fast and hard. He would have to back off. At least a little. He tried again. "Aren't you bored living in a small mountain community?"

Sunny shook her head, her love of her surroundings shining through. "I love the warmth and the sense of community here in Carlisle."

"Is that the only reason you stay? For family?"

"My grandfather needs me to help run his business," she said.

"Surely he could hire a plant manager."

"He doesn't have to, not when he has family." Sunny got up and retrieved the peach cobbler Matilda had baked for them. "Do you want ice cream with this?" she asked.

Zach knew exactly what his new bride was doing. "Waiting on me, or just trying to change the subject?" he drawled.

Sunny flushed. She stacked two desert plates on top of the ice cream, picked up the cobbler with her other hand and carried it all to the table. "I don't see you volunteering much about yourself," she asserted as she sat down again.

"That's because your life sounds like more fun," Zach said as he finished his dinner and helped himself to dessert. "So, tell me more about this class. What are you going to learn?"

Sunny toyed with the cobbler on her plate. "I don't know yet."

Leaning close, Zach noticed the faint blush of freckles across her nose. "Why would they think you need it?"

Sunny rolled her eyes and dropped her fork. "You have to ask after those getups they caught us in?"

Zach grinned at the exasperation in her tone. He knew how much the locals loved Sunny. This gift was something special. Obviously they had given it to her for a reason. "You haven't answered my question," he teased.

"They know I love to learn."

"And how do they know that?"

She drew a deep breath and looked him straight in the eye. "Because I delayed taking over my grandfather's company for two years, until I had gone back to school and earned an M.B.A."

"You didn't feel comfortable taking it over with just him to guide you?"

"No. I'm the kind of person who likes to be well versed in whatever subject I tackle before I dive into it."

"Hmm...I'm just the opposite. I tackle something first, then read the directions only if I can't figure it out on my own."

"I figured as much."

"So how long is this class going to take?" Zach didn't want it to take up too much of her time, since she already seemed quite busy at the factory. Besides, the house was lonely without her.

"I have five lessons and a graduation party, spread out over the next couple of weeks. Each class is supposed to be an hour or so in length."

"You're going alone?" If it was down the mountain somewhere, maybe he could drive her.

"No. Five other women have signed up to take it, too."

"Don't they already know how to be loving wives?"

"They hope to learn something. And so do I," she said firmly.

"To use on me?" Zach asked hopefully.

"No way." Sunny rose gracefully and carried her dishes to the sink. "I signed up to learn something that will help me when I really give my heart to someone and get married."

That wasn't the welcome prospect it should have been, Zach thought as he began to take care of his own dinner dishes. Instead of feeling relieved to know that she one day intended to end this farce of a marriage to him, as promised, he felt a flash of jealousy. Determinedly he pushed the feeling away. What she did was no business of his. He'd been hurt to the quick when Lori had died; his pain had intensified when he'd become involved with Melody; he wasn't going to open himself up to that kind of pain again. Not for Sunny, not for anyone.

"IS EVERYONE ready for lesson number one?" the instructor asked.

As ready as I'll ever be, Sunny thought, settling into a folding chair in the community church basement. Booklets stamped *How to be a Loving Wife* were passed out. Sunny stared at the cover, taking in the photo of a bride being scooped up in her husband's arms. If only married life were that simple, she thought wistfully. She sighed. Life with Zach was much more complicated than she had anticipated.

"Sunny, what did you and your husband have for dinner tonight?"

Sunny offered a mortified smile. "Casserole that was brought to us over the weekend."

"Describe how the table was set, what your centerpiece was and any special touches you added, like sprigs of mint."

Sunny shrugged. "I didn't set the table. We took what we needed to the table with us. And each did our own dishes afterward."

A gasp of dismay was uttered by the entire group. Sunny looked at them. "I am not waiting on him hand and foot."

"Then how do you expect him to ever want to wait on you?" the instructor asked gently.

"I don't!" Sunny said, flushing all the more as she recalled Zach bringing her the supper tray up to her room the first night they were married. She had yet to pay him back for his thoughtfulness. And that made her feel guilty.

"One kindness begets another, Sunny," the instructor said sternly. "Now, please, try to keep an open mind...."

ZACH AWOKE the next morning to the delicious smells of bacon and hot coffee. He shifted onto his stomach, his arms and legs hanging off the rollaway bed, and buried his face in the pillow. No doubt Sunny had made just enough for herself again. "She sure knows how to torture a man," he grumbled to himself.

"I beg your pardon?"

Zach rolled over with a start. Sunny was standing in the doorway with a tray in her hands. He shook his head to clear it, sure he must be dreaming. "Breakfast in bed?"

"Well, I'm in a hurry. I have to get to the office, and you weren't up yet," Sunny explained. She marched in as crisply as her fuzzy bunny slippers would allow.

Zach caught a drift of her perfume—it was lemony this morning—as she bent to help him put a pillow behind his head and settle the tray on his lap. She looked very sexy in a business suit. "Did something happen I'm not aware of?" he asked.

"If you think this is payment for staying out half the night, you're wrong," she said.

Was that a tinge of jealousy in her voice? "I was over at the clinic, reading files. Now that people are coming to see me, I figured I should be more up on patient history.''

"Sure you just didn't want to avoid seeing me?"

Zach shrugged, aware she was looking at his bare chest and the sheet that came *almost* to his waist. He knew what she was thinking: he wasn't wearing much. Considering the way his body was reacting to her nearness, Zach shared her wish that he had on more than his glen-plaid boxer shorts. He yanked the sheet up to cover his navel and ran his hands through his hair. "I wasn't sure what kind of mood you'd be in after you took that class, so I thought I'd make myself scarce."

"As you can see, Zach, my mood is fine."

That was a question open for debate. She was serving him breakfast in bed, but she didn't look happy about it. "So why are you waiting on me hand and foot all of a sudden?" And why did she look so damn cuddly and kissable, even in her ultraconservative business attire?

"Can't you guess?" Sunny took a small notepad from the pocket of the frilly gingham apron she had tied around her waist. "It's an *assignment*."

"Oh." Zach's spirits took a nosedive. He had hoped that she had done this out of the goodness of her heart. In retrospect, he could see how irrational that hope was. Sunny didn't believe they were really married any more than he did. She wasn't interested in playing house, either. Never mind having the kind of hot, passionate fling with him that he wanted to have with her.

"So?" Sunny stood poised with her pencil over the pad. She eyed him expectantly.

Zach nudged his sheet a little higher, so it rested against his ribs. He leaned back against the pillow and the wall casually. "So what?"

Color stealing into her cheeks, Sunny blew out an exasperated breath. "Make some inane comment about what I've just served you, Zach."

He looked down at the tray and couldn't help but be pleased by what he saw. The French toast was golden brown, perfectly prepared and dusted with confectioner's sugar. The bacon was crisp, the orange juice chilled, the coffee black, strong and steaming. She had even put a flower from her garden out back in a vase. "Breakfast looks wonderful, Sunny," he said softly, meaning it.

"'Breakfast...looks...wonderful...Sunny,'" she murmured as she wrote. Finished, she gazed at him and offered an officious smile.

"Now what are you doing?" he asked dryly.

"Making notes, of course, for my report back to the class. I found out last night that every lesson has a homework assignment. We all have to do them and report back to the class on the results of our assignment."

Now, this, Zach thought, sounded like trouble. "What other kind of assignments are you going to be asked to do?"

Sunny looked bewildered. "I don't know."

"Give me a hint." Zach cut into his French toast.

"I wish I could, but I truly don't have a clue. Our instructor wants to surprise us. Now, do you have any other comments to make about breakfast?"

"For you to write down?" he asked, feeling a wave of orneriness coming on.

"Yes," she said primly, her pen at the ready.

"Well, the food is delicious."

"'The...food...is...delicious....'"

"But it doesn't look—"

"'Doesn't look—'" Sunny was so busy writing she didn't see him get out of bed.

"Nearly as delicious as you," Zach said, taking her into his arms, so that her hands and the notepad were trapped between them. She smelled and felt as delicious as she appeared.

"Zach—" Sunny's soft voice carried a warning, as did her stiff, unrelenting posture.

"Hmm?" he asked. Taking advantage of her inability to move, he feathered light kisses down her nape.

"Don't." She shifted against him restlessly, her breath hitching in her chest.

Zach's heart started a slow, heavy beat as he studied her upturned face. "Why? Going to put this in your report, too, Sunny?" he asked, hoping he could make her understand how foolish and invasive of their privacy this class was.

Sunny drew an indignant breath and stomped on his bare foot with her bunny slipper. He let her go. Grinning, he got back into bed. Sunny in a temper was something to see.

"You think I won't write this down, don't you?" she said sweetly.

"Which part? Where I kissed your neck or you stomped on my foot?"

"I'm writing them *both* down."

Oh, no. Zach could feel another lecture from a well-meaning patient coming on. "Both?" he croaked unhappily.

"Of course my stomping on your foot was done accidentally—" Sunny continued blithely.

Like hell it was, Zach thought. Not about to let her know she was getting to him, he kept his face expressionless. "Accidentally on purpose, you mean," he corrected.

"But—" Sunny ignored him and kept writing furiously "—it was enough to spoil the mood." Finished, she grinned victoriously. "There. I completed my assignment. It didn't work, despite my very best efforts, which you, Zach, can attest to if asked. And our marriage is still doomed! Perfect!"

Zach shook his head. "You want to fail?"

"Of course," Sunny said smugly, closing her notebook with a snap. "Don't you?"

ZACH WAS STILL asking himself that question as he let himself into the clinic. He knew he should want to fail at this marriage business. Failing at it would give him and Sunny both an easy out. But failing—at anything—went against his grain. He didn't like playing games. Whereas like a chameleon, Sunny excelled at them. He wondered why she would put up with this, then determined he would find out.

In the meantime, it wouldn't hurt to keep her off her guard, Zach thought. She'd caught him by surprise, serving him breakfast in bed. He could do the same, too. Put her in a position where she didn't know what to think, either. Besides, if she could tell everyone he had sent her flowers, maybe the nosy townsfolk would get the idea that things between Sunny and him were fine and they would stop pushing them to become the perfect newlywed couple. It was worth a try anyway, Zach thought.

He reached for the phone book on his desk and thumbed through the Yellow Pages. There were three florists in the vicinity. He was trying to decide which one to use, when the door to his office banged open. Sunny's grandfather stood in the portal. As usual, he was dressed in his fishing apparel.

"I ought to shoot you on sight," Augustus Carlisle said.

"What for this time?" Zach asked.

"Breaking my granddaughter's heart—that's what!"

Zach frowned. "What are you talking about?"

Augustus shook his finger at Zach. "She's over at the factory right now, locked in her office, and she won't come out, and all on account of you."

"Did she say what I'd done?" Zach asked curiously as he folded his hands behind his head. No doubt about it. Sunny was a woman who was full of surprises.

"No. But it was clear to the women who work with her that it had something to do with that class on marriage they're all taking down at the church." Augustus peered at him suspiciously. "One of them said she mighta been trying out some sort of lesson on you. Did she?"

"I think that's a private matter, best left between Sunny and me," Zach said calmly.

Augustus sent a fulminating glance at Zach, then just as abruptly became more reasonable. "I understand that Fergus was over here yesterday, offering you some advice."

Zach took his feet off the edge of his desk and put them back on the floor. "He told me to send her flowers."

"And did you do it?" Gramps pressed.

"No." Not then, Zach added, but right now he had been about to order some. And not because Fergus had told him to do so.

"So what stopped you?"

Zach shrugged. "Unlike Sunny, I don't like to be told what to do," he said emphatically. "*Especially* in my private life."

Augustus's eyes narrowed to slits. "You know, I should have taken my shotgun to you while I had the chance. But for whatever reason my granddaughter has taken a shine to you, and the two of you are married, so I won't."

"Gee, thanks," Zach said sarcastically.

"I will, however, insist you do something to cheer her up. We can't run a business if she is locked in her office."

Then maybe you should take that up with Sunny, Zach thought as the outer door to the reception area opened. Zach saw a mother with twin babies troop in. Deciding the only way to get rid of Augustus Carlisle was to agree with him, he said impatiently, "Look, I'll order flowers and give them to her this evening."

Augustus assessed Zach with a frown. "You'd better do it right, son," he warned.

Zach gave Augustus a flip look. "Is there any other way?"

Augustus scowled. "In the meantime, I have something to discuss with you. Do you still want to give me a physical?"

"Yes."

"Then let's get down to it."

Augustus was already unzipping his fishing vest. Zach led the way to an examining room. The next twenty minutes were spent obtaining a complete medical history, the fifteen after that doing an exam.

"So how am I?" Augustus asked when Zach had finished listening to his heart and lungs.

"On the surface, everything's fine, but something has to be causing these chest pains you've been having."

"How do you know I'm still having pains?"

"I know because you're here, asking me to examine you. If you weren't, you'd likely put it off another month or two." Augustus said nothing to disagree. "So when were the last ones?" Zach asked.

"Last night, when I got back from the stream. I was cleaning some fish for dinner and the pain went from here—" Augustus pointed to his chest "—all the way down my left arm into my hand."

"Sounds scary," Zach said.

"It was. *Is.*"

"How long did the pains last?"

"Only about five or ten minutes. They quit after I went over and sat down."

"What about the fish?"

"I put it away, to finish up later. I figured maybe I'd overdone things, so I went to bed early. I felt a lot better when I got up this morning."

"But you're scared the pains will come back."

Augustus nodded grimly. "That's why I'm here. What do you think it could be? Angina?"

"It's possible. To say for sure, we'd need to admit you to a hospital and do a complete series of tests."

Augustus vetoed that. "I don't want Sunny upset."

"We can do this without her knowing," Zach said calmly.

Augustus hesitated. "You promise you won't breathe a word of this to my granddaughter?" Zach nodded. "Okay, then do it," Augustus said.

Zack picked up the phone and began to make arrangements. Half an hour later, it was all set. Augustus would have the necessary tests done at a hospital in Knoxville, the following week. A physician friend of Zach's would personally oversee Augustus's care. Sunny would never know anything, at least while the tests were being done. Afterward, when a diagnosis was made, Zach would use every means at his disposal to persuade Augustus to tell Sunny what was going on.

Zach spent the day seeing a steady stream of patients. By the time five o'clock rolled around, he was pleasantly tired. He hadn't felt such a sense of satisfaction since arriving in Carlisle, he thought, as he took off his lab coat and loosened his tie. The only thing he hadn't done was call the florist. But he figured they had to have something in stock. When he reached the door to the florist, he swore softly in frustration. A big Closed sign hung on the door. Zach peered inside. The lights were off. The building appeared empty. Now what? he wondered.

It was too late in the day to order from the two other florists on the mountain, and they were probably closed up, too.

Augustus drove up in his big black Cadillac sedan. He rolled down a window on the passenger side. "I figured you'd forget," he said.

"I didn't realize the florist closed so early." Even as Zach said it, he knew it was a lame excuse. He should've taken care of this earlier.

"Yeah, well, I owe you a favor anyway." Augustus thrust a large ribbon-wrapped box at Zach. "Sunny's favorite—yellow roses." He rolled up his window and roared off.

Zach went back to his brand-new pickup truck and drove home. Sunny was dropped off right after him. She got out of Matilda's car, briefcase in hand, then waved as Matilda drove off. She looked tired and frazzled after a day at the office. She saw the florist's box and instantly became wary. Zach suddenly felt as tongue-tied as any kid. Wordlessly he handed the box to her.

"Where did this come from?" she asked, in a voice that sounded oddly rusty.

You don't want to know, he thought guiltily, and wished like hell he had followed through on his initial instincts and done this himself early that morning. But he hadn't, so he would just have to make the best of it. "Open it and see," he said.

Sunny put down her briefcase and struggled with the ribbon. She gasped as she pried off the lid and saw the two-dozen roses inside. "Oh, Zach," she said, her voice choking up even more. She looked up at him, eyes glistening. "Yellow roses are my absolute favorite! How did you know?"

Zach shrugged, feeling even guiltier. "Your grandfather." And that was true, he reassured himself. There was no way he wanted Sunny to know how she had really happened to get this beautiful bouquet tonight.

"I'll take them inside and put them in water," she said.

"Want to go out to the diner to eat?"

Again she looked surprised. "Well...I guess we could. Zach, are you sure? Eating out is going to be like being on public display again."

"We don't have anything to hide," he said gruffly. "Besides, maybe it's time people got used to seeing us together." Maybe it was time he and Sunny got used to being together.

"Well, all right, but I want to change into something more comfortable first." Sunny flushed the moment the words were out.

For once Zach passed up the opportunity to put a sexy twist on her utterance. He nodded. "I'll go out and get your mail for you."

He was surprised to find his own mail in the box, as well. He hadn't changed any of his addresses. Leave it to Fergus to go ahead and do it anyway, Zach thought.

Minutes later, Sunny bounded down the stairs in jeans, sneakers and a white long-sleeve T-shirt. She had a pretty blue sweater tied around her neck, to ward off the chill of the spring evening. She had taken her hair down, and it fell over her shoulders in a riot of glorious red-gold curls. Irritated to find his heart slamming against his ribs, Zach stood and offered her a casual smile. "Ready to go?"

"Yep. I just want to run the casserole dish over to Matilda before we go, okay? You can wait for me in your truck. And grab up my mail, will you? I want to read it on the way to the diner."

"Pretty good at giving orders, aren't you?"

"You could say that!" Sunny bounded out the kitchen. The back door slammed.

Zach locked up and went out the front. He slid behind the wheel and waited. To his relief, she wasn't long in returning. To his dismay, she no longer looked the least bit happy. In fact, he thought as she neared, there was a decidedly militant edge to her posture. "What happened?" he asked as she climbed in stiffly beside him.

Sunny swiveled to face him. "What do you think happened?" she shot back, so angry she was trembling. "I know the truth about the flowers, Zach!"

Chapter Five

Roses in the Fire

"Zach, how could you?" Sunny stormed.

He braced one hand on the steering wheel and cautioned her with the other. "Whoa, now. Just hold on. It wasn't my idea."

Sunny lifted a brow skeptically, recalling, Zach supposed, just how difficult it was to get him to do anything against his will. "Well, it was and it wasn't," he amended hastily. "I was going to send you flowers—"

"Because Fergus told you to send them," Sunny declared sagely.

Zach paused. "You know about that, too?"

"Aunt Gertie can't keep her mouth shut—never could. And what do you mean do I know about that, too? What else should I know?"

Zach swore and said nothing. He was in up to his neck now.

"Zach, you better tell me. If I find out any other way—" Sunny warned, eyes flashing.

Zach knew there would be hell to pay. "I got the flowers from your grandfather to give to you."

"So they weren't from you after all." Sunny's expression saddened even more.

"No."

"So why did you pretend they were?" she asked, visibly upset.

"Because sometimes honesty isn't the best policy."

"Oh, really." Sunny surveyed him with glacial cool.

Zach regarded her in exasperation. "Haven't you ever kept something—some bit of information—to yourself because you knew it would hurt the other person?"

His words struck a nerve. She had done just that the day she'd met Zach, in not admitting up-front that she knew who he was, which made her as guilty as he was.

"Besides, I didn't want to hurt your feelings, and you had already assumed that the flowers were from me before I got a word in edgewise, so I went along with it."

Just when Zach thought he was getting through to Sunny, she abruptly got angrier.

She shook her head at him and studied him grimly. "I can't believe it. I can't believe my past is repeating itself this way!" She slammed out of the truck.

Zach vaulted out after her and followed her halfway up the drive. "What are you talking about?"

Sunny stopped so suddenly their bodies nearly collided. She pivoted to face him. "My parents did the same thing to me." New color swept into her cheeks. "They had my nanny or their secretaries buy presents for me because they could never remember, or make the time, to go shopping themselves."

"They *told* you this?" Zach was shocked.

"No, of course not," she said, her eyes gleaming with suppressed hurt. "But I caught on eventually. Kids have a way of sensing things."

Zach couldn't imagine growing up like that. His parents had always taken special care choosing gifts and he had learned to do the same. Which made what he had done to Sunny even worse. There was only one remedy for this. He would have to find some way of doing something special for her... all on his own.

Zach took her hand and led her over to the front porch. "What happened when they realized you knew what was going on?"

"They stopped pretending and gave me money, instead, to spend as I chose." Sunny sat down on the steps.

Zach followed suit and took her into the curve of his arm. "Did that make it easier? Or worse?"

"A little of both, I suppose." She rested her head on his shoulder. "It was a relief knowing I didn't have to pretend they'd put any thought into anything. But it hurt knowing they couldn't spare the time."

"I'm sorry," Zach said. Sorry he'd taken the easy way out with the flowers.

Sunny straightened and shook off his sympathy, her expression determined. "I shouldn't complain. My parents are good people and they work very hard. If they'd had less-demanding jobs, maybe it would have been different for me."

And maybe it wouldn't have, Zach thought. Maybe this was the key to Sunny's heart and soul, the reason she not only tolerated, but seemed to relish, the community's interference in their lives. "Tell me how it was," he encouraged softly, lifting her chin to his, wanting to know more about what had caused the glimmer of hurt in her eyes.

She looked deep into his eyes. "What do you want to know?"

"Were you an only child?"

Sunny nodded, still holding his gaze.

"You said you had a nanny," Zach continued softly, covering both her hands with one of his.

"A succession of them, actually, from the time I was born." She tightly enmeshed her fingers with his, then went back to resting her head on his shoulder.

"Why more than one?" Zach used his free hand to stroke her hair. It felt like silk beneath his fingertips.

Sunny snuggled closer. "We moved around a lot. You name it, I've lived there. They could never find a governess willing to travel around with us for more than a year or so at a time, so when one left, another came in to replace her."

"How long did that continue?" he asked quietly.

"Until I was twelve. Then I went to boarding school in Switzerland."

"Where did you go to college?" Zach asked, liking the way she felt in the curve of his arm.

"Where my mother went for undergrad, Smith. Wharton School of Business, for my M.B.A."

"Prestigious schools," he commented, impressed. "Your parents must be very proud of you."

Sunny shrugged. Lifting her head, she drew back again. "I really don't want to talk about this any longer."

He could see the walls around her heart going up again. It surprised him how much he wanted to tear them down. Usually he took his cues from other people. If they didn't want to talk, he didn't push it. But with Sunny, he couldn't help it; he had to be closer. "Why not?" he asked.

His question was met with silence. With every second that passed, Zach could feel her drifting further away from him. He wanted desperately to keep her near, so he tried once more. "What's your relationship with your parents like these days?"

"I'm not close to them, okay? Now, can we just leave it at that?" she asked impatiently, aware she was trembling with unresolved emotion.

Zach's expression was concerned. "On one condition," he drawled, as the two of them squared off.

Sunny lifted her chin contentiously. "What condition?"

He smiled and took her hand in his. Time to enact part two of figuring out what made his new wife tick. "That you have dinner with me tonight, just as we planned."

"THIS ISN'T going to work!" Sunny said outside the diner. She didn't even know why she had agreed to come here with him, after the flower fiasco, except that dining out would be much less intimate than eating at home.

"Sure it'll work. All we have to do is pretend to be cooing lovebirds and word will get out that we don't need any more help in the romance department. Everyone will back off. Then we won't have any more problems like the one we had today with the flowers," Zach said.

He was doing it again, Sunny thought. Realizing intuitively where she was vulnerable, then attempting to somehow attend to all her hurts, past and present. Because he was a healer by profession? Or because there was something special between them? She only knew for sure that the more he learned, the closer she felt to him. If they kept on this path she was going to have a hard time resisting him when he did make his move for her. And she felt sure that it would be very soon. Sunny backed up slightly on the sidewalk. "I'm no good at acting."

"So don't act," Zach said with a shrug. "Just be nice and remember the way you looked and felt when I kissed you the other night."

That was the problem, Sunny thought. She couldn't get those kisses out of her mind!

"Okay, so wing it," Zach advised cheerfully under his breath.

"Better." That matter settled, she breezed through the diner doors.

Rhonda-Faye looked up from behind the counter. Sunny knew, from the flushed, yet pale, color in her friend's face that something was wrong. She slipped onto a stool in front of Rhonda-Faye. "You feeling okay?"

Rhonda-Faye nodded. "Just a little backache—that's all."

Zach sat down beside Sunny in a drift of wintry cologne. Suddenly he was all physician. "Any contractions?" he asked.

"No. Besides, I'm not due for another week, Doc."

Zach quirked a brow. "Babies have been known to come early."

Rhonda-Faye rubbed at her lower back. "Truth to tell, I wouldn't mind having the birth over with, but I'm not in labor, not yet anyway."

"Think George is going to do any better this time?" Sunny asked, recalling how excited Rhonda-Faye's husband tended to be at times like this.

Rhonda-Faye shook her head. "Heaven only knows. Though he's promised me this time he is going to stay calm."

Zach frowned. "Isn't this your fourth child?"

"Yes, and you'd think George would be used to the whole birth process by now," Rhonda-Faye drawled affectionately. "But you never know."

Sunny grinned. If Zach was around for the birthing of the baby, he was in for a real surprise. "You seem to need to get off your feet anyway," Sunny said. "Why don't you go on home and let me take over tonight?"

"What do you know about running a diner?" Zach interrupted.

Sunny gave him an incensed look. "I've helped out before. Haven't I, Rhonda-Faye?"

"You saved my life last Labor Day weekend, when two of my high schoolers came down with chicken pox at the same time. But really—the two of you being newlyweds and all—I couldn't impose."

"Sure you can," Zach said genially. "You go home and rest and Sunny and I will take over here. I'm sure we can handle it."

Rhonda-Faye squeezed Zach's arm and leaned over and gave Sunny a hug. "I'll pay you back," she promised. With a grateful nod at them both, she grabbed her sweater and slipped out the back door.

"Mighty sweet of you," Zach said, stepping behind the diner counter.

Sunny tied on an apron as two families with young children walked in. "You ain't seen nothing yet." She met Zach's eyes, stunned at the easy way she and he had slipped into couple mode. "You want to take the orders, while I fill the plates?"

Zach grinned. "Only if you promise not to break any over my head."

"Very funny. The booster chairs are in the back."

The next few minutes were a flurry of activity. Sunny was surprised to see that Zach was no novice when it came to waiting tables. He got the two families situated and took their orders in a jiff.

Circling back around to the grill, he said, "Two burger platters, cremated, extra grass. Both kids want short stacks and Grade A and their mom insists on side dishes of whatever fruit we've got to go with it."

Sunny poured silver dollar-size puddles of pancake batter onto one end of the griddle, then added two hamburgers to the other. "Applesauce and milk are in the fridge."

He whisked over to give the family their drinks, the kids their dishes of fruit, then swaggered back to Sunny's side, looking as at home in an apron as he did in a white lab coat.

"We're running a little low on draw one," Zach reported softly. "Harlan down at the end is going to be wanting more." His breath brushed her hair as he watched her slide perfectly made pancakes onto two kid-size platters, then reach over and flip the sizzling burgers.

"Harlan always wants more coffee," Sunny said. "He works the night shift at the factory." She handed the kiddie platters over to Zach, unable to help but be both pleased and surprised at the eager way he had pitched in. She never would've expected it of him. But then, maybe she just hadn't given him a chance. She had to admit the skunk incident had gotten them off on the wrong foot. And that in turn made her wonder what their relationship would have been like if they had met some other way.

The bell over the door tinkled as another group of customers walked in, pulling Sunny from her trance. Telling herself sternly that this was no time to start getting warm, fuzzy feelings about her new husband, she forced herself to snap out of it and said, "The coffee is down below the coffeemaker."

"No problem," Zach said.

He chucked her under the chin, then bent to press a light, fleeting kiss on her lips. Her mouth was still tingling as he drew back.

Eyes still holding hers, he said softly, "I'll get the fire going under it right away."

The coffee wasn't the only thing with a fire under it, Sunny thought with a rueful grin, as she continued to run the grill while Zach waited tables.

When closing time rolled around, she was pleasantly exhausted. Zach pulled the shades, switched off the outside lights and locked the door, as Sunny dished up the last of the day's chili, two generous salads and warmed a slab of Rhonda-Faye's homemade sourdough bread. She settled in a booth in the back, while Zach dimmed the lights and fed quarters into the jukebox. Seconds later, the lively sound of Robben

Ford and The Blue Line singing "Start It Up" filled the room.

The music Zach had played made her want to get up and dance. She was tapping her foot to the jazzy rhythm as he brought two frosty mugs of root beer to the table and set them down.

Before she knew what he was doing, he had pulled her up out of the booth, and they were jitterbugging to the bluesy beat. Eyes locked, bodies moving in synch, they spun their way through the song.

Breathlessly they returned to the booth.

"Thanks for helping out," Sunny said, as she slid in opposite him. "I'm sure Rhonda-Faye appreciated it."

Zach nudged her foot with his. "What about you?"

"Fishing for a compliment?" she teased.

"More like trying to find out if you're still mad at me over the flower business."

"Ah, yes, the yellow roses." She squeezed his hand. "What do you say we go home and throw them in the trash and start over, as friends this time?"

Sunny knew she wanted to give him a second chance. "But if we're going back to square one, we don't know very much about each other," she said cautiously, aware her heart was thundering against her ribs.

He focused on the turbulence in her eyes. "What do you want to know?"

Everything, she thought. Sunny smiled. "Have you ever been tied to a community before?"

He pinned her with a look. "I have a fondness for Murfreesboro, where I grew up, and Nashville—because I went to med school and did my residency there—but I don't particularly need to live in either place to be happy, if that's what you're asking," he said.

It was. Sunny suppressed her relief. "What about your romantic past? Have you ever been deeply involved?"

He nodded grimly. "Like you, I was engaged once."

Compassion welled up inside her. "What happened?"

"I knew from the beginning that Melody was close to her family. In fact, her abiding love for them was one of the things that attracted me to her. What I didn't realize until after we became engaged was how totally dependent she was on them. Everything that happened in our life together was somehow dictated by her family. She couldn't buy groceries without consulting her mother first. Needless to say, planning the wedding was a nightmare, finding a place to live even worse. I realized I couldn't live that way. I needed a wife who would put our relationship first, a woman who would make our marriage a priority and not just a convenience. With Melody, it was never going to be like that, so we broke it off."

Sunny knew firsthand how devastating it was to end an engagement, even when you were sure you had no choice. "That must have been a difficult time for you," she said sympathetically.

Zach nodded. "My own parents understood, of course. Hers didn't."

Sunny grinned. "Another sign you weren't meant to be together, I guess." She lifted the mug of root beer to her lips. "I think I'm going to like being friends," she said softly. She certainly understood him a lot better.

"Me, too," Zach said quietly. He leaned back against the booth and studied her.

Sunny knew he was thinking about kissing her again. Unbidden, the image of Zach as he had been that morning came to mind. Wearing nothing but his glen-plaid boxer shorts, his long, strong body stretched out sexily on his uncomfortably small bed. Just looking at him had made her heart pound and her mouth go dry. When he'd kissed her, her senses had gone into an uproar. They were still topsy-turvy every time she was near him.

As for her fantasies, Sunny knew she didn't need to be asleep to dream of what it would be like to be led down that forbidden path and be made love to by Zach.

Sunny drew a tranquilizing breath. With effort, she forced herself to put her daydreams aside and concentrate on the reality of the situation, which was that he didn't love her. And without love, any passion they shared would be meaningless.

She had waited too long to indulge in meaningless sex—with anyone, even her husband. She cleared her throat, determined to keep them on the right track. "Zach—"

"I know."

He touched her face with the palm of his hand, and it was all she could do not to lean into the incredible warmth and gentleness of his caress.

"Friends," he said, keeping his eyes locked on hers. "For now."

The way things were going, Sunny wondered how long they would stay that way. Because despite their efforts to keep theirs a marriage in name only, they were getting closer to making love every moment they were together.

EXHAUSTED FROM her impromptu stint at the diner, Sunny was sound asleep when the telephone rang. Groggily she pulled the receiver into bed with her and mumbled a sleepy hello. "Sunny? It's George! Get Zach on the line! Quick!"

"Hold on." Recognizing the panic in George's voice, she put the receiver down and stumbled into Zach's room across the hall.

Hand clamped to the smooth, warm skin of his muscular shoulder, she shook him out of what appeared to be a sound sleep. "Zach, wake up! Rhonda-Faye's husband is on the phone."

"Thanks, Sunny." Clad only in his boxer shorts, he shot out of bed and moved across the hall. "George, what is it?" He listened intently, then said, "Calm down. Everything is going to be fine. Just get Rhonda-Faye in the car...no, don't bother to get her dressed...and meet me at the clinic as soon as you can. I'll be there in five minutes. Bye."

"Rhonda-Faye is in labor?"

Zach nodded, already striding back across the hall to retrieve his pants. "Apparently her water broke about fifteen minutes ago. The contractions have been going on ever since. George says they are about a minute and a half apart."

"A minute and a half!"

"Yeah, I know. At that rate, they'll never make it down the mountain to the hospital. Looks like I may have to deliver her baby in the clinic." Zach tugged his zipper up, slid his feet into his Topsiders and pulled on a shirt.

Sunny grabbed the clothes she'd worn earlier and slipped on her shoes. "You'll need help." Her clothing bundled in her arm, she raced down the stairs after him. "I'm going with you."

SUNNY DRESSED in the pickup on the way over. They had just opened up the clinic when George pulled up in his Suburban. "Where's Rhonda-Faye?" Sunny asked, since George appeared to be alone.

"Maybe lying down in back?" Zach suggested with a shrug, already circling around to help.

George grabbed a suitcase and hopped out. He was red in the face and completely out of breath. "I got here as soon as I could!" he yelled.

"You did fine," Zach said. He peered into the middle seat. It was also empty. "Where's Rhonda-Faye?"

George looked inside the vehicle, then back at Zach. His expression was panicked. "Oh, my God—"

"You forgot to bring her?" Zach guessed.

George nodded. "I was in such a hurry to get here—"

"Calm down, George," Sunny said.

"It's going to be fine," Zach reassured him. "You drive back and get her and Sunny and I will go into the clinic and call Rhonda-Faye to let her know you're on your way."

George nodded, still looking completely in a dither. "Right." He put the suitcase back in the car, climbed behind the wheel and took off.

"The way George is acting, you'd think he was a first-time father," Zach mused, swiftly unlocking the clinic door.

Sunny grinned. "Rhonda-Faye says she gets more worried about him than delivering the baby."

Zach chuckled and shook his head as he headed for the phone. "Rhonda-Faye? Doc Grainger here. George is on his way back to get you. How are you doing? Every minute and fifteen seconds now, hmm? How long are the contractions lasting? Three minutes. Yeah, I agree—it'd be ridiculous to try to make the trip to the hospital at this point. No problem. Sunny's here with me, so she can help handle George. I'll see you in a few minutes." Zach hung up. "Looks like we're going to deliver a baby."

While Sunny kept an eye out for George and Rhonda-Faye, Zach spread out the sterile sheets and brought out the emergency incubator. Sunny gasped as the Suburban pulled up. "Zach, Rhonda-Faye is driving!"

Zach rushed out with her. George was sitting in the passenger seat beside his wife, a bloody cloth pressed to his head.

"He fell!" Rhonda-Faye said.

"I was running up the front steps to get her," George explained through gritted teeth.

Zach helped Rhonda-Faye step down from behind the wheel. Perspiration matted the hair on her forehead. She was pale and trembling. "Ohhhhhh," she moaned, doubling over as another contraction hit her.

"Rhonda-Faye, honey?" George said, sounding even more panicked as he stepped down, too.

"Zach's got her," Sunny said. She wrapped a steadying arm about his burly waist. "Let's just get you both inside."

NO SOONER were they both inside than Rhonda-Faye let out a yelp. "The baby's coming!"

"Now?" George said, looking as if he were going to faint.

Sunny pushed him into one examining room, while Zach helped Rhonda-Faye into the other. There was another scream from Rhonda-Faye. George went even paler. Sunny guided him to the examining table. "Lie down before you fall down, George."

He groaned, even as he complied. "Rhonda-Faye—"

"Zach's got her. I'm sure they're doing fine." Struggling to recall what first aid she could, Sunny removed the bloody cloth from George's temple. The bleeding had stopped, but it was clear from the depth of the cut that he was going to need stitches.

She reached for a packet of sterile gauze and ripped it open. "I'm going to put a bandage on your head and then I'm going to go in and see if Zach needs any help. Okay?"

"Okay."

"You just stay here until Zach can get to you."

Hurriedly Sunny covered the gash on George's forehead. She patted his arm reassuringly, then dashed into the other examining room just as Rhonda-Faye let out another strangled sound. A sterile surgical gown tossed on over his clothes, Zach was sitting on a stool in front of Rhonda-Faye.

"Now," Zach said calmly, "one more push. C'mon, Rhonda-Faye. You're doing fine. Help me out here. Push. . . ."

Rhonda-Faye bore down with all her might. The next thing Sunny knew Zach was holding a new baby in his hands. Sunny's eyes filled with tears as the baby let out a healthy squall of outrage.

"It's a girl, Rhonda-Faye," Zach said, laying the feisty newborn on the sterile cloth draped across her mother's stomach.

"Oh, she's beautiful," Rhonda-Faye gasped, gathering her close.

"That she is," Sunny agreed emotionally, as Zach swiftly cut the cord. Sunny grabbed a sterile gown to wrap the baby in, while Zach tended to his patient. "And she'll be even prettier once we get her cleaned up."

"One bath and a set of soft, warm clothes coming up," Zach promised.

"Oh, take her in to let George see first," Rhonda-Faye asked.

Zach smiled at Sunny and nodded his approval.

"Time to go see your daddy," Sunny said. Gently she lifted the baby in her arms. She carried the bundle in to George. He took one look at his beautiful new daughter, then fainted dead away.

"You sure you're doing okay now, George?" Zach asked as he and Sunny escorted the trio out to the Suburban, where a neighbor was waiting to drive the happy family home.

"You mean except for the splitting headache and the six stitches in my temple?" George asked, tongue in cheek. Now that all the excitement was over, he had calmed down swiftly.

"I don't know why he fainted," Rhonda-Faye said. "It's not as if we haven't been through all this before."

"I think it was the way the baby looked," George said. "All that goo she had on her—"

"That was the vernix caseosa," Zach explained. "It covers the skin and protects the baby in the womb." Zach paused. "You were never in the delivery room before?"

"He was afraid he would faint," Rhonda-Faye said, and they all laughed.

"You call me if you have any problems today, and I'll stop by your house this evening to check on you all," Zach said.

"Thanks, Doc," Rhonda-Faye said.

"Thank God you were here tonight," George said. "We sure are lucky to have you here."

"I'm glad I was here, too," Zach said.

Zach and Sunny waved as the couple drove off. Together they walked back into the clinic and began to clean up and tidy everything. When they were finished, Zach put a pot of coffee on. They each filled a mug and went outside to sit on the back steps. Five in the morning, the stars and the moon were still visible. Sunny was as charged up as he could ever remember seeing her. Zach was wired, too.

It wasn't supposed to be like this. They weren't supposed to act like two members of a well-rehearsed team. They had signed on for a marriage of convenience with little or no exchange of feelings, yet almost from the moment he'd met her, his emotions had soared out of control. The medical emergency tonight had shown him yet another side of her.

She would, Zach decided, someday make some man a very good marriage partner. The only problem was, he realized uncomfortably, that he didn't want to think of her married to anyone but him.

His feelings puzzled him. After his engagement to Melody had ended, he had sworn never to get involved with a woman who put friends and family ahead of her relationship with him. Yet there he was, getting more and more tied to Sunny with every second that passed, knowing all the while that she cared every bit as much about the opinions, needs and wants of her family and friends as Melody had. Knowing that, he should have been running as fast and as far away as he could, but he didn't want to lose or halt what had begun between them.

"Is that the first time you've ever seen a baby born?" he asked. She was sitting so close to him he could feel her body heat.

"Yes. It was amazing, wasn't it?" As Sunny turned partway to face him, she nudged his muscular thigh with her knee. Her eyes were bright with wonder. "I mean, you always hear about the miracle of birth and all that, but to actually see it, be a part of it..." Aware she was rambling, Sunny stopped. Aware her knee was touching him, she pulled back.

Zach didn't want them to stop touching. He smiled at her and linked hands so that their fingers were intertwined. It was all he could do not to pull her into his arms and make love with her then and there. "I feel the same way," he admitted huskily. "Life is very precious." Drawing a breath, he gazed at the ever-lightening sky overhead. "I don't think any of us ever realize how much so except for times like this, when we're witness to a new life or—" Zach blinked and his voice thickened revealingly as pain exploded deep inside him "—we see one taken away."

"It must be hard for you when a patient dies," she said softly.

Zach nodded. He pushed the difficult memories away. "Losing someone close to you is hard on everyone," he said huskily. But he didn't want to talk about that, he thought as he wrapped an arm affectionately about her shoulders, squeezed and pressed a kiss into the fragrant softness of her red-gold hair. "Thanks for helping me out tonight. I don't know what I would have done without you."

"All a part of being a doctor's wife, I guess," Sunny said. "At least, a doctor's wife in a small town," she amended hastily, then paused.

Leaning her head on his shoulder, she noticed that Zach was still looking extraordinarily thoughtful, almost moody, tonight. She wondered if he was thinking about another patient of his, one he perhaps hadn't been able to help.

Straightening, Sunny took another sip of the hot coffee. Cupping both hands around the stoneware mug for warmth, she asked, "Did you mean what you said to George and Rhonda-Faye earlier—about being glad you were here?" *With them and with me?*

Zach turned to her. He knew a lot was riding on his answer. The first pearly-gray lights of dawn filtered over the horizon, illuminating his handsome face. The brooding look of moments before vanishing, he cupped her face in his hand. "Yes," he said, brushing her lips with a brief, all-too-fleeting kiss. "I did."

Chapter Six

Better Your Heart than Mine

"No, I understand, Gramps. Of course I can ask Zach." *I just don't want to,* Sunny thought. This morning, in front of the clinic, Zach had almost kissed her. If he had, she was sure they would have succumbed to the passion simmering between them and made love. He'd known it, too. He'd also probably known the reckless, highly romantic nature of their moods had come not from the joy they were finding in being with each other or their pretend marriage, but from the romance and excitement of delivering a baby into this world. And that excitement would fade, Sunny told herself severely. And when it did they would still have to live in the same house every day. And they would still be married.

"Yes. I'll see you in your office around ten. And I'll have the sample pages for the new mail-order catalog with me."

Sunny hung up the phone. She turned, to find Zach lounging in the doorway of the kitchen. He was dressed for work in shirt, tie and jeans.

"Ask me what?" he said.

"Nothing."

"C'mon, Sunny," he demanded impatiently.

"Gramps can't give me a ride into work, and it's so late that Matilda has already left."

"And you still can't drive your Land Rover because the skunk smell is still in it."

"Right."

Exasperation glimmered in his eyes. "If you need a ride, why didn't you say so?"

Because I'm beginning to feel too close to you, Sunny thought, a little desperately. "I didn't want to impose."

"You wouldn't be imposing."

The look in his eyes almost had her believing it. Sunny tapped a high-heeled foot against the parquet floor. "I need to fix that skunk smell."

Zach's expression softened sympathetically. "You've already tried damn near everything, haven't you?"

Sunny nodded, embarrassed. Zach had been right about that; they shouldn't have gotten into her vehicle until they had rid themselves of the smell. She shrugged and held the sample pages of the catalog to her chest. "Everyone says to just give it time."

"Time can work wonders in lots of areas," Zach agreed with a teasing grin, as his gaze roved her slender form.

He was thinking about kissing her again. Sunny could tell by the gleam of anticipation in his eyes. Her heart racing, she sidestepped the sensual embrace she sensed was coming if they dallied any longer. She was *not* going to be foolish enough to fall in love with him, not when she knew he couldn't wait for this farce of a marriage to end. Keeping her back to him, she gathered up her belongings. "I'm in a hurry, Zach," she said impatiently.

When she looked around at him again, he grinned, not the least bit put off by the edginess in her tone.

"And testy, too."

"I can't help it." Picking up where she'd left off when the phone had rung, Sunny swept a brush through her hair with long, practiced strokes. "It's aggravating me to no end not having a car to drive. I'm used to being completely self-sufficient."

Zach watched as she clipped her hair at the nape with a gold-filigreed barrette. "I know what you mean. I'm a pick-up-and-go type of person myself. In med school, my ability to leave town for a weekend now and then was the only thing that saved my sanity. I still like to get away for a weekend when I can."

"Where's your favorite place to go?" Sunny asked curiously, applying lipstick to her lips.

"I like water. Lakes and streams over beaches, generally. They're less crowded and I prefer the country to the city any day when looking for a little R and R." Zach watched as if mesmerized as she pressed her lips together to set the lipstick. "What about you?" His eyes trekked slowly back to hers.

"I don't know." His face was inches from hers as she recapped her lipstick and put it back in her purse. "I never really take vacations per se." Although Zach was making her regret that, too.

"How come?" He stepped behind her. Placing his palms on her shoulders, he kneaded the tenseness from her shoulders.

Sunny leaned into his soothing touch and briefly closed her eyes as his stroking, massaging fingers worked their magic. "Habit, I guess. As a kid, I saw plenty of the world, since my parents worked all over Europe, but every trip was always combined with work somehow. They'd go off to meetings. I'd either tag along and read a book while they labored and negotiated, or go tour a museum with my nanny. Either way, it seemed more like an extension of my education than a vacation." Relaxed now, she leaned against him.

Zach's hands stilled and he pressed a kiss in her hair. "Maybe that's why you're so crazy about those old 'I Love Lucy' reruns, like the ones you were watching last night before bed. If there was any fun to be had within a hundred miles, Lucy would find it," he said as he wrapped an arm around her waist and held her near.

Sunny grinned, enjoying the warmth and gentleness he exuded. "You're right about that."

His arm still hooked around her waist, Zach turned her to face him. "A little zaniness is good for the soul," he said, looking down at her affectionately.

Sunny felt her resistance to their marriage fading, inch by precious inch, even as they strayed into uncharted territory. Zach was becoming genuinely fond of her, as she was of him; that was not her imagination. "And you're the expert on zaniness, I suppose?" she teased back, thinking that if ever she had longed for her Ricky Ricardo, she had found him in Zach.

"Damn straight I am. Furthermore, one of these days I'll show you how to take a long, lazy weekend where nothing at all productive gets done."

"Sounds fun."

"In the meantime, I'll drop you at work," he said, handing her her purse and briefcase and tucking her arm in his.

Sunny looked up at him and saw something—a feeling, an emotion—that she couldn't analyze. "Don't you have to be at the clinic?"

Zach's eyes glinted with good humor. "I think I can be fifteen minutes late arriving one morning. I'll just put a note on the clinic door telling people when to expect me."

He was still going way out of his way. Sunny dug in her heels, afraid that if he evidenced much more kindness she really would be head over heels in love with him. "You don't have to do this for me, Zach."

"Yes, I do, Sunny," he replied, tightening his hold on her possessively. "You're my wife."

"WHAT'S GOING ON?" Zach asked as he pulled his pickup into the Carlisle Furniture Factory parking lot.

Sunny groaned as she looked at the fifty or so employees scattered in front of the building, now interestedly gazing their way. "I completely forgot. It's Earth Day and the local chapter of the Sierra Club always comes out and celebrates by planting a tree."

Zach didn't mind the two of them being seen together. In fact, he was beginning to kind of like it. But it was apparent Sunny did mind. He brought the truck to a halt. Leaving the engine running, he put the vehicle in park, then turned to her. "Looks like we have quite an audience," Zach murmured mischievously, unable to resist teasing her. Maybe it was time he stopped fighting it and played his husband act to the hilt. As long as they were together, they might as well have a little fun, he thought.

"Well, not to worry. There's not going to be anything for them to see," Sunny announced.

"On the contrary, Sunny," Zach drawled as he gave in to the temptation that had been plaguing him all morning and took her by the shoulders and kissed her soundly. Finished, he lifted his lips from hers and sifted a hand through her hair, knowing even as he did that he would never get enough to satisfy him, not even if he kissed her a thousand times. "I think there should be quite a lot for them to see. We are newlyweds, after all."

Sunny regarded him with a steamed glance, resenting, Zach supposed, the easy way she surrendered to him whenever he took her into his arms. What she didn't realize was that the feeling—of surrendering beyond their will—was mutual and just as difficult for him to fight. "I should have known you'd take advantage," she huffed.

Zach raised his brow, his desire to possess her, heart and soul, growing all the stronger. "Sunny, honey, that wasn't taking advantage," he murmured playfully. "This is."

Before Sunny had a chance to draw a breath, he had pulled her back into his arms and slanted his mouth over hers. Their kiss was hot and sweet and completely overwhelming in its intensity. Apparently forgetting her decision not to give an inch where he was concerned, she wreathed her arms around his neck and met him halfway. Engulfed by a wave of passion and need long held at bay, she let him pull her closer, deepen the kiss to tempestuous heights. Time lost all meaning as emotions swirled, and still it wasn't enough, Zach thought, amazed and shaken. It would never be.

He hadn't meant for this to happen. But now that it had, he was having a difficult time stopping himself. Only the thought that they had an audience kept him walking the straight and narrow. With difficulty, he ended the kiss, and lifted his lips from the tantalizing softness and warmth of hers.

She released a shaky breath. "You're not playing fair," she accused, her eyes shooting indignant sparks while she gave him an otherwise adoring look that was strictly for the benefit of their audience.

She wanted to talk about fair? Zach thought, still caught up in the moment and the essence that was her. There was nothing fair about this situation they found themselves in. Nothing easy about the circumstances that were compelling him to fall in love with her.

He cupped a hand under her chin, enjoying the slightly bedazzled state she was now in as much as he had loved leading her there. He tweaked her on the nose. "I never play fair, Sunny."

"WELL, LADIES, ready for lesson number two?" the instructor asked.

"If you ask me, Sunny's lessons are already working," Matilda said. "You should have seen that kiss Zach gave her in front of the factory this morning. Whoo-eee! It nearly knocked my socks off!"

"Thank you, Matilda," Sunny said dryly. She felt herself flushing bright red.

"Now, Sunny, don't you go getting embarrassed on us," Aunt Gertie counseled. "What you and Zach have is something to be proud of, to savor!"

"I agree," the instructor said, "and that is the basis for your next lesson. There is nothing sexier or more compelling to a man than the feeling of being the lord and master of his own castle. I am telling you, ladies, let your man take charge on the home front, and he will reward you with kisses galore."

"That's ridiculous," Sunny said.

"I don't like the sound of that, either," Matilda said.

"Let's put it to the test and then see," the instructor said. "Here is your assignment. I want all of you to give your husband free reign over his home for a period of six hours, starting tomorrow evening after work. His every wish is to be your command. You are to anticipate his every need. And most important of all, you are *not* to tell him or anyone else what you are doing or why. Not even a hint."

"Why?"

"Because if we tell them, they'll take advantage of us," Rhonda-Faye grumbled.

"Close, but no cigar," the instructor said. "Quite simply, if your husband thinks this is a game, he will treat it as a game. And this is serious, ladies. I am teaching you a whole new way of life."

"I don't know about the rest of you, but I did not sign on to learn how to become slave labor," Sunny said.

"I don't want you to be a slave," the instructor corrected. "I want you to treat your husband like a king. And when you do, you will find out that he will of his own volition treat you like his queen. Naturally, I'll expect you to keep a diary of your efforts and the results. During the next lesson we will share them with the class."

Sunny groaned, anticipating Zach's reaction. Could it get any worse?

SUNNY EMERGED from the kitchen just as Zach walked in the front door. His glance slid over the navy silk lounging outfit she had just put on, then moved to the yellow roses prominently displayed on the pedestal table in the front hall.

"Are those my flowers?"

"Yes. They are."

He narrowed his eyes at her. "I thought you were going to throw them out."

"I decided it's the thought that counts," Sunny said cryptically. In this case, she wanted everyone to think she cherished the flowers. Whereas in truth, she was using them for a little visual on-site reality check. No more getting caught up in the idea of playing husband and wife the way she had in front of the factory this morning. No more steamy kisses. No more pent-up desire. No more falling in love with Zach! She was going to forget what they were teaching her in that class and live in the real world. And the reality was, no matter how tantalizing the idea of being really married to Zach or making wild, reckless, passionate love with him, neither thing was going to happen. Therefore, the only way to protect her heart was to keep her emotional distance.

Zach set down his medical bag with a thud. "What's going on here, Sunny?"

She regarded Zach innocently. "I'm trying to be nice," she said breezily. "So play along with me. Now, what would you like for dinner?"

"You're offering to cook for me?" He regarded her skeptically.

Sunny felt ridiculous, like a character out of some fifties sitcom trying to please her man. She wet her lips. "If you like." She was hoping desperately he had other plans.

"Uh-huh. What are my choices?"

Sunny shrugged, the irony of the situation not lost on her. She was married to the man and she had no idea what he liked. "Fried chicken. Steak on the grill."

Zach's lips compressed into a thoughtful line. "Fried chicken takes a while, doesn't it?" he prodded.

"Yes."

He faced her, an eyebrow raised in question. "Aren't you tired?"

Never too tired to make you happy, dear—at least, for the next six hours. "It'd be my pleasure," Sunny said, sidestepping his question altogether.

"To serve me?" Zach countered with a penetrating look. "I don't think so," he said drolly. "What's going on, Sunny?" He closed the distance between them and pointed to the yellow roses. "Are you trying to pay me back for the flowers mistake?"

"No, of course not." Sunny flushed.

"Then why the sudden eagerness to please me?" Zach towered over her. "Gramps going to pop in or something?"

"Not to my knowledge," she said truthfully, then pivoted. "I'll go start dinner."

Hand on her shoulder, he tugged her back to his side and gently spun her around. "I haven't decided what I want yet."

"Oh." Sunny folded her hands primly in front of her and took a deep, calming breath. "Right."

His eyes gleamed with mischief. "You know what? I think I'd like prime rib."

Leave it to Zach to make things more difficult, she thought. "I don't have any, but I think I can get to the market before closing. Unfortunately," she murmured, "it's not the sort of thing our butcher usually carries."

"I guess fried chicken will have to do, then," Zach drawled.

Sunny smiled and didn't comment. Every time she commented she got herself into trouble. Deciding this assignment would be a lot easier if they spent a few minutes apart, she said, "The newspaper is in the living room, dear."

Zach gave her a testing glance. "My slippers, too?" he asked innocently.

Sunny paused. As far as she knew, he did not wear slippers. But she supposed, for the sake of the class, she could give the idea some play. "I haven't seen your slippers."

"If you had, would you go get them?"

This assignment was a killer. "If you needed me to get them," Sunny specified sweetly. She couldn't think of a single reason where that would be the case.

Aware he was still ruminating over the sudden change in her behavior, Sunny slipped into the kitchen.

To her chagrin, he joined her there.

While he removed his tie and unfastened the first two buttons on his blue-and-white striped cotton dress shirt, Sunny got out the chicken.

He watched as she rinsed and patted it dry, pulled out the seasoned flour, then beat an egg and milk into a frothy mixture.

Zach poured himself a glass of iced tea as she prepared the chicken.

"You've done this before, I presume?" he said finally.

Sunny nodded, not shy about admitting, "Many times."

"Who taught you?" he asked softly, drawing closer.

"I taught myself by reading cookbooks."

His eyebrows lifted. "Julia Child?"

Sunny's mouth curved wryly as she added oil to the skillet and waited for it to heat. "Try Betty Crocker, Fannie Farmer, Pillsbury and anyone else who specializes in home-style cuisine. Since my parents preferred nouvelle cuisine and continental fare, I wanted pizza, hog dogs, fried chicken, grits and so on."

"Naturally." Zach grinned.

"What did you grow up eating?"

"Home-style American cuisine."

Sunny dropped pieces of chicken into a black cast-iron skillet. "What did you want?"

Zach stood looking over her shoulder. "Home-style American cuisine."

Satisfied the chicken was cooking nicely, Sunny went over to the pantry. She contemplated various side-dish possibilities. "Mashed potatoes okay with you?"

"As long as you make gravy. I can't eat mashed potatoes without gravy."

Sunny chuckled at the absurdity of that. Finally a character flaw she could identify with, she thought. She had begun to think Zach hadn't a whimsical bone in his body.

"Want me to make a salad to go with it?" He started for the refrigerator.

Sunny intercepted him midway. Zach's helpfulness was not in her lesson plan. "No. I have to do it," she said quickly, before she could think.

Some of the pleasure left his eyes. It was replaced swiftly by hurt. Sunny could have shot herself for the slip.

Zach folded his arms in front of him calmly. He quirked a brow. "What do you mean you have to do it?" he echoed.

Sunny flushed. Now that he was alerted to her deceptiveness where the evening was concerned, he would never just let it go. Nevertheless she tried to bluff her way out of trouble. "You know what I mean."

"I'm starting to." He trapped her against the refrigerator door. An arm on either side of her, caging her in, he murmured silkily, "If I didn't know better, I'd think you'd do just about anything to please me tonight."

Sunny inhaled jerkily. Unable to move without bringing them into closer contact, she remained motionless and held her ground.

"That's it. Isn't it?" Zach asked.

Their earlier camaraderie vanished. Hurt shimmered in his eyes, turning them an even darker blue.

"This is some sort of lesson . . . an experiment for your class."

"Now, Zach, I'm just trying to be cordial," Sunny said breathlessly.

He studied her. "Suppose I told you I'd changed my mind about the chicken and now I wanted steak."

Sunny kept her eyes on his. "Then I'd finish the chicken, save it for tomorrow and heat up the grill in the meantime."

"Hmm." Zach strode away from her and retrieved his glass of iced tea. "I think I will read that paper."

Sunny couldn't believe he was just going to walk away from her, now that he knew what her task was, but he did. Heart pounding, she waited for him to come back, to deliver the next zinger. He did neither, and she spent the next hour in the kitchen alone, preparing dinner, while he watched the television news and read the paper.

This proves he is definitely not husband material. No, she corrected herself wearily, her innate sense of fairness coming to the fore. It just proves he doesn't like to be a lab rat for some how-to-be-happily-married class. And for that, Sunny couldn't blame him.

"YOU REALLY OUTDID yourself with dinner," Zach said, after they had finished their strawberry shortcake and coffee. And that was a surprise. He had half expected her to ruin it on purpose, after he'd caught on to the reason behind her sudden change of heart.

Fool that he was, he had thought it was due to the passionate kisses they'd shared, the fact that they were getting to know each other and more often than not now liking what they found. He should have known that the idea of Sunny meeting him halfway to try to make this temporary marriage of theirs work was too good to be true. She had been forced into it, too. She also had to deal with that class. But that didn't excuse what she'd done this evening, raising his hopes unfairly by dressing in that silky navy blue outfit that made the most of her slender curves.

"Thank you," Sunny said politely. "I'm glad you enjoyed dinner."

Not as much as I'm going to enjoy this, Zach thought. Deliberately he let his eyes drop to her breasts before returning to her face. "You know what I really feel like doing?"

Sunny flushed. "The dishes?"

"No, Sunny," he drawled, sitting back in his chair. He folded his arms in front of him. "I think the dishes can wait indefinitely, don't you?"

Her tongue snaked out to wet her lower lip. "What did you have in mind, then?" She kept her eyes on his.

"I want to play a little game," Zach said, testing her reaction, and finding it every bit as uncertain and off kilter as he'd hoped.

"I've got Scrabble upstairs," Sunny said, already jumping up to get it.

Zach caught her wrist as she passed by. "I want to play Simon Says," Zach announced. He tugged her down onto his lap. "And I want to be Simon."

"That's a child's game."

"Not the way I intend to play it."

Muttering something indecipherable, Sunny attempted to vault off his lap but was held in place by his arms. "Darn you." She tried to release his arms from her waist. Failing at that, as well, she wiggled around to free herself, then stopped seconds later, apparently realizing what her subtle shifting was doing to his already much-aroused lower half. She drew a deep breath, the silk shifting beneath her thighs, and began in a much more reasonable tone, "Zach. I don't think—"

He touched a gentle hand to her lips, silencing her. He was aching all over and was sure he would pay for this hours later in terms of pent-up need, but he was not willing to stop until he had given Sunny a taste of her own medicine. "So you're refusing to do what I say—is that it?" he asked mildly. He knew how she liked to succeed at whatever she did, even the meddlesome class. In fact, he was counting on that trait in her to get them back to a level playing field, where honesty of feelings and not silly games prevailed.

Sunny flushed guiltily. She drew another bolstering breath, glanced down at her watch, as if contemplating how much time she had left on this particular assignment. "I thought you might want to rent a movie," she said finally.

Zach shook his head. Watching a video would do nothing to get Sunny to drop the compliant-wife act. "I think I'd prefer the game."

She bit her lip and looked up at him. He knew what she was thinking—that Simon Says, in the hands of a lascivious male, could be dangerous. "Shall we give it a try?" he asked softly, in a tone meant to incense her. "Or are you afraid to play games with me?"

Her temper visibly igniting, Sunny glared at him. "I am not afraid," she announced loftily.

"Good, then let's give it a try," he said, ready to get down to business. "Simon says put your arms around Zach's neck."

Sunny's eyes darkened angrily, as they always did when she was forced to do something she did not want to do, but she followed his instructions.

Zach smiled. Lucky for her, he had scruples. "Simon says close your eyes."

Rebellious color flooded her pretty cheeks, but she reluctantly lowered her thick red-gold lashes anyway, closing them almost all the way.

Zach frowned. "Are you cheating?"

"What?"

"Sunny, c'mon. Close those eyelashes all the way, now," he commanded sternly. "If you're going to play this game with me you have to play it right."

Murmuring a protest, she frowned nervously and started to shut her eyes completely. "Aha," Zach announced victoriously, "caught you!"

"Caught me!" Sunny echoed, incensed, as her eyelids flew open.

Zach shook his head at her in mocking report. "Simon never said you could open your eyes, either," he teased.

Her cheeks burning as she realized she'd been duped, Sunny pummeled his chest with her fist in aggravation. "This isn't fair!"

"No, Sunny, it's the way the game is played." Zach put his hands around her waist and started to shift her off his lap before any real damage could be done, any real temptation succumbed to. "You lose." *In fact, because of your playacting tonight, we both do.*

To his surprise, she refused to move in the direction he wanted her to go. Instead she remained squarely on his lap. Her lower lip was thrust out in a seductive pout. Her breasts were rising and falling seductively with each breath she took.

"I want another turn," she demanded stubbornly.

As Zack felt the warm, silk-clad weight of her settle in more comfortably on his lap, it was all he could do not to groan aloud in frustration. He had known all along how she hated to lose. He had even suspected she might purposely lose the game quickly, just as a way of getting out of having to play. He hadn't figured she would get genuinely flustered so soon, lose and then insist on playing another round.

"Sure now?" Zack taunted, no more willing to lose face than she was. "I could confuse you even worse this time," he warned.

"Just start playing!" she ordered bad-temperedly. "Now!"

"Okay." He grinned, keeping his hands around her slender waist, as he orchestrated a quick end to the game. "Simon says touch your lips to mine." His whole body throbbing, he waited for her to leap off his lap.

But this time, to his dismay, Sunny kept her cool. She quirked a brow. "You think I won't do it, don't you?"

Zach ignored the urgent demands of his body and gave her a look. "Babe, I know you won't do it."

"Ha! Just goes to show what you know!" Sunny muttered. Anger sparking in her eyes, she leaned forward and lightly touched her lips to his.

Zach knew what she was expecting. She was expecting him to play around a little more.

In truth, he had initially intended to do just that. But there was something about the softness of her lips against his, the cozy feeling of having her on his lap, that sent the rules of the game—and caution—to the wind.

He knew he shouldn't do it. He no longer gave a damn. Wrapping a hand around the back of her neck, he tilted her head beneath his. Their lips fused. He felt the need pouring out of her, mingling with the desire and the temper. And beneath that, he felt the tenderness that was so much a part of her, too. His need to be close to her was as overwhelming as it was magical. He threaded his fingers through her red-gold hair, tipped her head up to allow himself greater access, and claimed her as his.

As her mouth opened to his, he kissed her long and hard and deep. He kissed her until she moaned softly and melted in his arms. Until it felt as if they were both on a long magic-carpet ride. Realizing it was either stop now or take her to bed—and she wasn't ready to be made love to, at least not yet—Zach slowly, reluctantly, drew the kiss to an end.

His mouth tingling, his whole body trembling, he moved back slightly. He expected to see fury in her face. And he saw it, but only after the wonder and the stars in her eyes faded. "Guess I got a little carried away," he drawled.

"I guess you did," Sunny said, almost too sweetly.

And once again, to Zach's acute disappointment, she reined her feelings in.

"But then," she continued, gazing up at him with all-too-innocent eyes, "that kiss you gave me is nothing that can't be remedied."

"Remedied?" He did not like the sound of that.

"Sure," Sunny said, as she slid gracefully off his lap. "Because now it's my turn to play Simon."

Zach shrugged. "Give it your best shot."

"Simon says stand on one foot."

Zach rolled to his feet and stood on one foot.

"Put both feet on the floor."

His expression benign, he remained on one foot.

She looked him up and down, like a farmer examining a prize bull at market. Zach's feelings of unease increased. He sensed she was about to order him to take a long walk off a short pier.

"Simon says...turn toward the back door."

Keeping his shoulders loose and relaxed with effort, Zach turned casually toward the back door. No need to let her see she was getting to him, he thought.

Her smile widening, Sunny dropped her voice a seductive notch. "Simon says turn toward the sink."

He turned toward the sink.

"Simon says wash the dishes!"

It was all he could do not to groan. There were a lot of dishes.

"And Simon says don't stop until you're done!"

Sunny threw a napkin at him and stomped out of the room.

His body still humming with unslaked desire, Zach watched the provocative sway of her retreating backside. Maybe he had overdone it, but it sure had been fun while it lasted.

Chapter Seven

Ain't Misbehavin'

Zach awoke at dawn to the sound of water hitting metal. He looked outside to see Sunny in cutoffs and an old Smith College sweatshirt, hosing down the *inside* of her Land Rover. Finished, she tugged a red bandanna bandit-style over her mouth and nose, picked up a bucket of soapy water and a scrub brush and leaned into the Land Rover.

Pulling on a pair of running shorts, T-shirt and shoes, he headed downstairs. He heard Sunny swearing her displeasure as he neared. The top half of her was inside the truck; her bottom half extended out of it. As Zach neared her, he couldn't help but notice what spectacular legs she had. Or how much he liked seeing her in those Daisy Mae short-shorts she was wearing.

Sunny let out another litany of swear words as she continued to scrub her vehicle's interior carpet.

"Need any help?" he asked.

She started, and would have bumped her head if Zach hadn't caught her in time. She pivoted toward him, her bare legs rubbing up against the length of his. "Must you always sneak up on me like that?" she demanded.

"Do you have any idea what time it is?" Zach countered, his nose wrinkling at the pungent smell.

"Six-fifteen." Sunny shot him a look that told him she still hadn't forgiven him for kissing her so thoroughly during their Simon Says game.

Aware he wasn't due over at the clinic until nine, he stuck his hands in his pockets and lounged against the side of the truck. "Don't you have to go to work today?"

"Don't you?" she retorted, without bothering to answer his question.

So she wasn't going to make it easy on him. Zach rubbed at the stubble on his unshaven jaw. He felt just a little contrite, even though he didn't really believe he had anything to apologize for. Sunny had only gotten what she'd had coming to her for trying to put one over on him. But, as always, she didn't see it that way.

Aware the silence between them was growing, he drawled, "So what are you doing out here?"

"Trying to get the skunk smell out of my Land Rover. What are you doing out here?" she asked in a muffled voice.

Enjoying the view, Zach thought. Trying to make peace. "Checking up on you."

"Well, as you can see," she said temperamentally, letting go of the bandanna, so that it fell around her neck, "I'm fine!"

Zach didn't think so. He pushed away from the rear of the vehicle and ambled closer. "Need a hand?"

Sunny shrugged. "Be my guest and scrub away."

"What are you using this time?" he asked. She had done this at least every other day since they'd imbued her Land Rover with the fragrance of skunk. She had also air-dried it in the sun repeatedly, also to no avail.

"I think a more apropos question is what haven't I used. Today it is a solution of detergent and water."

Zach wrinkled his nose. "I hate to say this, but so far it doesn't seem to be working."

Sunny scowled and dipped her brush back in the bucket. "You got any better ideas?"

"Actually...yes."

She straightened, hands on her hips, and gave him an expectant look. "I'm all ears, husband dear."

"What do you say we hand wash the whole interior in tomato juice?"

"Because the tomato juice would also stain the carpet."

"So rip out the carpet and forget about it. The seats are leather, so the tomato juice will rinse right off."

Sunny studied the sudsy carpet on the floor of her truck. "I don't know, Zach. It seems like a waste."

Zach understood her reluctance to spend money unnecessarily. He also knew, in this case, that it was going to be inevitable. "Have you tried your insurance?" he asked.

Sunny nodded unhappily. "My policy only covers theft, wrecks and natural disasters involving fire or flood."

"A skunk isn't a natural disaster?"

Sunny made a face. "Only to you and me."

Zach regarded her Land Rover. "Thought about driving it off a cliff? Then you could collect."

"Very funny and the answer is yes, numerous times." Sunny kicked at a tire. "Dammit Zach, I want a vehicle to drive!"

"You could borrow mine," he suggested gently.

Sunny shook off the offer. "You need it for house calls."

Zach sighed. "True."

She gave him another droll look. Moving several feet away from her vehicle, she fingered the bandanna she still had looped around her neck. "I think now is the point where you're supposed to say something soothing," she remarked, tongue in cheek.

Zach searched his mind for a comforting bromide to fit the bill. He couldn't come up with much. "Well, look at it this way, Sunny," he said sagely at last. "No good smell stays forever, so no bad smell can stay forever, either."

Sunny tilted her chin and kept her eyes on his. "Meaning what, exactly?"

Zach shrugged. "In a year it should smell better?"

Sunny closed her eyes and silently counted to ten. Finally she opened them again. "That's not helping," she said flatly.

Zach grinned down at her. "Then maybe this will."

He swung her up into his arms and carried her, protesting loudly all the way, over to her front porch. He set her down on the narrow steps.

"What do you think you are doing?" she demanded.

Zach touched the tip of her nose with his index finger, amazed at how much she had come to mean to him in so short a time and how dull his life was going to seem if he was ever without her again. "I'll continue scrubbing—it will be my good deed for the day. Now, sit here and be quiet for all of five minutes, okay?''

"I SAW Zach carrying you around this morning. My, the two of you certainly have a lot of energy," Matilda said, as she drove Sunny to work an hour and a half later.

Sunny knew she shouldn't have been laboring over her truck again before work, but she'd had to do something to use up the excess adrenaline pouring through her veins. She had barely slept at all last night, just thinking about Zach's kisses. Which were getting more and more frequent and potent all the time. She was beginning to seriously contemplate making love with him . . . to live dangerously for a change. She and Zach would never really be man and wife. They were just too different. But they could have a wild, reckless, passionate love affair. . . .

A love affair she'd remember and cherish the rest of her life. More important, she knew by the way he was kissing her, that he wanted to make love to her, too. So what was stopping her?

"Sunny?" Matilda said loudly, breaking into her thoughts. "You haven't heard a word I've said, have you?"

Sunny blinked. "Hmm?"

"Whatever are you thinking about?"

Zach, and how much I am beginning to care for him, Sunny thought.

"And why do you have that silly besotted look on your face?" Matilda continued, as she turned off

Main Street and onto the two-lane highway that led to the factory.

"I—" Sunny brought herself up short. "I don't know." She frowned. "I'm just worried about so many things." *Like getting out of this marriage with my heart and soul intact.*

Needing to change the subject, Sunny sniffed the inside of her wrist. "Do I smell like skunk?"

Matilda shook her head. "Apricot bath soap."

Now, there was a possibility she hadn't yet considered. "Hmm. Maybe I should try that on the interior of my car," Sunny mused.

"Maybe. Although I'm with Zach that nothing will get rid of a skunk odor when it gets on cloth or anything," Matilda said.

"We'll see," Sunny said.

Matilda gave Sunny a bluntly assessing look. "So how did your assignment go last night?" she asked casually.

Recalling how it had felt to sit on Zach's lap, her arms wreathed around his neck, and kiss him like there was no tomorrow, Sunny flushed. "We're not supposed to talk about it until class, remember?"

Matilda grinned. "He liked being king of his own castle, hmm?"

Heavens, yes! Sunny thought.

She turned toward Matilda, wondering if everyone else had gotten the same results from the experiment. "Did Slim?"

"He didn't notice anything different. That newly-wed husband of yours apparently did," Matilda said with a sly look.

"That's because Zach notices everything." Even more telling, Sunny thought, was the fact that she noticed everything about him, as well. Including the fact that he was much too big for that rollaway bed he was sleeping on in the guest room.

Knowing he was uncomfortable every night made her feel so guilty she'd begun to consider solutions. And she knew what Zach wanted, of course—to move into her bedroom.

ZACH REALIZED something was going on the moment he walked in that evening and saw the disassembled cardboard furniture boxes littering the front hall. He took the stairs two at a time, strode past the folded-up rollaway bed he had been sleeping on and skittered to a halt in the guest bedroom doorway.

Sunny was home and still dressed in the tailored green tunic and black skirt she'd worn to work. Oblivious to his presence, she was standing next to a maple bedstead that dominated the entire guest room, calmly unfolding a white cotton mattress pad.

Looking at the bed, Zach couldn't help smiling. "What's going on?" he asked laconically as he went to give her a hand.

"I know how uncomfortable you've been sleeping on the rollaway bed. And I've been meaning to do something about it," she explained, avoiding his eyes as she smoothed the mattress pad onto the bed, covering the gathered elastic corners on her side, while Zach wordlessly covered the corners on his side.

"So I brought home a new bed for you," Sunny said. "It's a double bed, which should be large enough for you to sleep comfortably on, I think. If you're sleeping alone, that is."

Enjoying the easy way they were able to work together, Zach helped her cover the mattress pad with a set of sage green cotton sheets. "How about if I'm not sleeping alone?"

Sunny gave him a droll look and tossed him a pillow. "Then it might be a little crowded," she said dryly.

She was determined, Zach thought, not to be anything more than politely friendly to him this evening. No matter what they had been through together bringing Rhonda-Faye and George's baby into the world, or the closeness they had shared afterward, or the way they had teased each other the night before. She was backing away again. Zach was not going to let her do that, even if he had to tease her mercilessly to draw her out of the cocoon she had woven for herself.

Anyone could know Sunny the public person. No one knew the private one. At least not the way Zach wanted and intended to know her.

He watched as she covered one pillow with a sage green case, then followed suit.

"Oh, I don't know. I think we could cuddle up on it quite nicely," Zach drawled. In fact, he could easily imagine making love to her on the thick new mattress.

Sunny sent him a sassy glance. "Dream on."

"Trust me. I intend to."

He dropped his pillow onto the left side of the bed. She dropped hers on the right.

"Okay if I try it out?" he asked casually, watching the way the late-afternoon sunlight drifted in through the windows, setting fire to her red-gold hair.

"Sure. I guess so. In fact, it's probably a good idea."

Zach kicked off his shoes and stretched out on the crisp, fresh-smelling sheets. Aware Sunny was watching his reaction to the bed closely, he frowned and asked, "Is this bed from the factory?"

"Yes."

Her expression became sober. Her teeth sliced into her soft, bare lower lip. For the first time since he had walked into the house tonight, she looked uncertain. He wondered if she was reevaluating the boundaries they had set out for their relationship, just as he was. He wondered, too, if she was beginning to feel as married as he was beginning to feel.

"It's one of the floor models for a discontinued Hearthside line," Sunny continued.

"Hmm." Zach closed his eyes and concentrated on the enormously comfortable feel of the bed beneath him. There was only one thing he needed to make this bed complete now.

He folded his hands behind his head and continued to study her. "What about the mattress and box springs?"

"They're from the factory, too. I bought the whole set at an employee discount." She leaned toward him to remove a tag that was still looped around the knobs on the headboard. As she moved, he was inundated with the fresh floral scent of her perfume. It was all he could do not to groan.

Tag in hand, Sunny straightened. She looked down at him, her eyes all at once businesslike and solicitous. Once again, he was struck by her innocence, and the lack of it in himself. It was impossible to go through what he had, not to mention what he had seen in the emergency rooms, and still retain any semblance of culpability. There was no fate or grand plan. Life was random. People did and said foolish things. And it was true, the worst things happened to the best people. Which was all the more reason he should have fun now, while he could, Zach thought, his playful mood returning full force.

"Why do you ask where the bed came from?" she inquired quietly.

"I don't know." Zach hesitated. Watching her, he could see she was determined to prove she could be in his presence and not react. Just as he was determined to prove that when in each other's presence, they couldn't help but react.

"I hate to say anything," he continued in a way he knew would provoke her curiosity and keep her there with him a little longer.

Sunny frowned. A tiny pleat formed between her eyes. "If there's something wrong with the bed you need to tell me, Zach."

He worked to suppress a wicked grin. He doubted she would like his analysis of what his new bed needed.

"Maybe you should just try it and see what you think," he said. Maybe then she would come to the same conclusion he had.

Ever the devoted businesswoman, Sunny assumed a worried look. She kicked off her shoes hurriedly and sat down on the edge of the bed, then, apparently unable to tell anything from that, rested her head on the pillow and stretched out. She wiggled her shoulders and hips slightly, testing the mattress beneath her for flaws. Finally she said briskly, "My side of the bed feels fine."

"Good."

"How about yours?"

"I don't know. I think there's something wrong."

"Where?"

Zach turned toward her a bit and patted the space next to him solemnly. "Here. Right in the middle."

"Are you serious?" Sunny sat up with a jolt. The idea that there might be something wrong with a product her furniture company manufactured was very alarming.

Zach shrugged in a way that allowed he was no expert when it came to furniture. "Maybe it's just me," he said. "You try it." He patted the mattress center. "Tell me what you think."

With a frown, Sunny scooted toward him a little more. Shoulders stiff, she lay back down. Again she wiggled her hips and shoulders, getting settled.

Watching her, Zach felt his mouth go dry. The loneliness he'd been feeling for months now intensified in a solid ache around his heart. He had never wanted to reach out to a woman more than he did at that moment.

"You know you're right, Zach." Oblivious to the swirl of feelings in his heart, Sunny stared up at the ceiling. "It is a little stiff," she decreed finally.

She wasn't kidding, he thought, as the ache in his lower half intensified by leaps and bounds.

A contemplative grin tugging at the corners of her soft lips, Sunny propped her head on her bent elbow and rolled toward Zach a little, so they were lying face-to-face. "But with any new bed there's always that breaking-in stage," she continued with the soothing zeal of a good furniture salesperson. Her eyes danced as she related, "Did you know that it can take up to three months to get to feeling really comfortable in a new bed?"

Zach grinned and Sunny blushed as they both became aware of the double meaning of her words.

"Oh, I don't know. I think I'm comfortable now," he drawled. "I think," he said as he gave in to temptation, pulled her into his arms and bent his head toward her softly parted lips, "all I needed—all I ever needed—was this."

Zach bent his head for a kiss. The feel of her lips beneath his was sweet, soft and all too intoxicating.

All too soon, Sunny broke off the kiss, her hand to his chest.

"Now, just hold on there a moment, lover boy," she drawled, gasping for breath. "This was not part of the deal."

But she liked it just the same. "I know." Zach grinned. "But maybe it's time we rethink our situation," he said.

Sunny regarded him suspiciously. "Rethink it how?"

Zach lay back on the pillow. He folded his hands beneath his head. "Maybe we should stop fighting what we're feeling."

For a second, Sunny looked tempted. She braced a forearm on his chest and rolled so that she was lying across him. "And what are we feeling, Zach?" she asked very, very softly.

He knew much depended on his answer. "For starters, a very strong, very undeniable attraction to each other." Unable to resist touching her again, he wound a curl of her silky red-gold hair around his fingertip.

Sunny leaned into his touch instead of away from it.

"I admit there's some chemistry," she said, surprising him with her honesty.

She looked down at his chest and tightened her fingers on the ends of his striped necktie. "But that doesn't mean we have to act on it."

Zach considered the way his lower body felt, the way she had responded to his kiss, trembling at just the mere touch of his lips to hers. They were fooling themselves if they thought they were going to keep this marriage of theirs platonic. It was time Sunny dealt with that fact, too.

He slid his hand beneath the veil of her hair and gently caressed her nape with his thumb. "We may not be able to help it, Sunny."

She bit into her lower lip tremulously, then gave him a smug look. "Oh, I think we will."

Zach felt another battle coming on, one he anticipated greatly.

"I don't know." He shook his head in exaggerated confusion, then teased, "We're living in extreme proximity, Sunny. We're married. Heck, who knows? Some night we might even find ourselves doing some lesson for one of your classes that involves us sharing the same bed."

The notion of them sharing the covers was apparently as disturbing to her as it was to him. Pink color climbing from her neck into her face, Sunny sat up. Swinging her legs over the edge of the bed, she turned her back on him. The fabric of her skirt pulled against her trim hips as she bent to retrieve her heels.

"I think I could get around any such lesson my instructor might cook up. Besides, I only have a few left."

Not ready to let her go just yet, Zach pried the suede shoes from her hand and shifted her so she was prone again and they were touching in one long, tensile line. "All the more reason we need to take things a step or two further and begin to explore some of what we've both been feeling," Zach said. "Because there's so much I want to learn about you, Sunny. So very, very much."

She was prepared to be drawn into his arms and kissed once more, but what she wasn't ready for was how fast she went from simply being kissed to kissing in return. She didn't even know how he did it. All she knew was that her world was taken over by the taste and touch and smell of him, that she'd never been so excited and that she felt wild and free and womanly for the first time in her life.

Giving in to the subtle pressure and gentle wooing of his lips, Sunny opened her mouth to the rapaciousness of his tongue and returned every touch and pressure tenfold. Before she knew it, one kiss had turned into many. It no longer mattered, she thought dizzily, as the yearning inside her, the sensation of being cherished, intensified into a fierce, unquenchable ache. All that mattered was that this touching, this tenderness, this gentle loving, never stop.

Zach groaned as she kissed him deeply.

Feeling the hypnotic stroke of his hands as they swept over her, Sunny started to succumb to whatever it was that came next. Then realized, as Zach began to unbutton her tunic, that no matter what he wanted, no matter how much she ached to be one with him, she couldn't give her body without also giving her heart.

For Zach, she feared, it was *not* the same. All too aware of the thundering of his heart and the rigid tension in his thighs, she tore her mouth from his and put a staying hand on his. "Zach, no. I—" The right time might come, but it wasn't here yet.

He sighed and released his hold on the button he'd been about to undo. "I was afraid you were going to say that," he murmured as he let her go.

Sunny studied him. Even though she'd said no to lovemaking, it was clear he was not giving up.

Zach touched a finger to her lips and gently wiped away the dewy residue of their kiss. He surveyed her tenderly. "You expect me to be angry with you for putting on the brakes, don't you?"

That was usually the drill, she thought. Say no to a man and he flew into a rage.

"Aren't you?" she asked curiously, still testing his reaction to her denial.

"No." Zach shook his head, his eyes glowing with pleasure. "I see this as a very necessary first step."

Sunny took a deep, hitching breath. A very necessary first step. To making their marriage a real one? "That sounds ominous," she quipped, aware her hands were trembling.

"Pleasurable," he corrected huskily with an unabashed grin. "And it will be, I promise."

Sunny was afraid of that, too.

She was irritated by the way she kept melting in his arms, despite all her intentions to the contrary. "I know you think so," she said tartly. She had yet to see. Yet to be brave enough . . . to go all the way. But Zach didn't know any of that. And she wasn't about to tell him. Her lips still tingling from his kisses, Sunny slipped away from him.

He relaxed against the pillows, making no move to follow her. "One of these days I'm going to get you back in this bed and we're going to find out what we've been missing," he teased. They were going to be together. It was only a question of when.

Chapter Eight

A Little Less Talk
and a Lot More Action

"Yes, sir. Absolutely. We'll have it to you within the month!" Sunny promised with a smile, then hung up the phone.

Matilda set a neatly typed list of new orders on Sunny's desk. "Good news?" she asked as she popped the lid on a can of diet cola.

"The best. Where's Gramps?"

Matilda picked up her steno pad. "Last I saw he was in his office, preparing for the sales meeting in the showroom this afternoon. After that, he's going fishing. You ready to dictate those letters yet?"

"Not quite. I want to tell Gramps my news first."

"Okay. I'll go back to figuring that new computer out. Now, that's a chore that should last me the rest of my life."

Sunny patted her assistant on the shoulder. Chuck Conway had been out three times to work with Matilda in the past two weeks, but she was still struggling to make the transition from one order-entry system to another. "Just keep at it. You'll get the hang of it yet."

"That I don't know about," Matilda murmured. "'Course, it might help if I actually read the instruction manual from cover to cover."

Sunny lifted a brow. "Any particular reason you haven't?"

"Yes. It's written in technogibberish. I don't understand a word of it."

Sunny grinned. "Think it'd be better if we hired Chuck to come in for a solid week, work with you and make up an emergency manual for you in language you do understand?"

"Maybe." Matilda tapped her pen against her steno pad. "I mean, I always get it when he's here. It's only when I try to work it on my own that I seem to get confused about what I'm doing and muck things up."

"I'll call Chuck again today," Sunny promised.

Sunny finished up her business with Matilda, then dashed off in search of her grandfather. Though she was now officially running the company, he still came in for a few hours every morning to lend a hand and answer any questions she might have. And the truth was, she liked having him around. He lent her plenty of moral support, and he believed in her gut instincts when it came to business, and her ability to manage the company. He also felt she was doing work she should be proud of. Sunny sighed, wishing everyone in her family felt the same way.

Her grandfather's door was slightly ajar. He had his back to her, but Sunny could see he was on the phone. Not wanting to interrupt, she lingered in the hallway.

While she waited patiently for him to finish, his voice floated out to Sunny. "That boy has a responsibility to this community, never mind my granddaughter! I don't want another doctor in Carlisle!"

Another doctor! she thought, straightening abruptly. Was Zach going somewhere? She could not recall ever seeing her grandfather look so angry.

Gramps glared up as Sunny slipped inside his office. He frowned. "I'm going to have to hang up. Yes, later." He put the receiver in its cradle. "What is it, darlin'?"

Sunny shut the door behind her. She stepped around the fishing gear that seemed to go everywhere with Gramps since his semiretirement. Hands shoved in the pockets of her trousers, she approached her grandfather's desk. "We won the bid. Carlisle Furniture is going to supply the beds, bureaus, tables and chairs for all the rooms of the new Southern Hospitality Inn in Nashville."

Gramps beamed and leaned over to give her a hug. "Congratulations, honey. I knew you could do it."

So had Sunny. If only her parents had the same confidence in her ability, she thought wistfully. "What was that all about—on the phone just now?"

"Nothing."

Sunny sent her grandfather a brief, dissenting glance. "It's not nothing if it's about my husband," she remarked sagely.

Gramps studied her. Without warning, his expression grew exceedingly grim. "You don't know what that rascal's up to now, do you?"

Sunny lifted her shoulder in an eloquent shrug. "How could I unless you tell me?"

"He asked for a transfer out of Carlisle."

The news hit her like a sharp blow to her chest, but she kept her demeanor impassive. "When?" Sunny asked quietly.

"A day after the two of you got caught draped in nothing but a chamois and a checkered tablecloth."

That fast, Zach had wanted the hell out of Carlisle. She had realized he had been unhappy about their predicament even before the two of them had been forced to marry. She hadn't realized he had put in for a transfer.

"And?" Sunny pressed for more details.

"And the person in charge of the physician recruitment program for rural areas called me to say they're still working on finding one."

"Why call you?"

"Because Carlisle Furniture chipped in on the moving costs for the new doc, remember? We'd have to pay moving and living for the new doctor. Not to mention recall the selection committee to review another round of appointments."

"Oh. Right."

Gramps stepped forward. "Everything okay?"

"Everything's fine," Sunny said, though she felt as though her whole world were coming apart.

"I take it Zach didn't mention this to you."

"No," she admitted tightly, doing her best to hide her inner misery. "He didn't."

"Yet another reason to wring his fool neck," Gramps muttered.

"Don't you dare," Sunny warned hot-temperedly. "I'll handle my new husband."

"Sure?" Gramps picked up the fishing lure he'd been working on while he was on the phone. He bent his head over it again. "I could talk some sense into him," Gramps offered slyly.

Sunny was hoping that wouldn't be necessary. "It may be he has already changed his mind about staying," she said optimistically.

Gramps's hands stilled and he looked up. "And if he hasn't?" he prodded with a frown, pausing absently to massage his left shoulder and the center of his chest.

Sunny drew a deep breath. "Then that's his decision." She wasn't about to force Zach into anything. Her parents had imposed their will on her; she was still reeling from the pressure. She wouldn't do the same to Zach.

Gramps surveyed her distressed expression. He set the lure in his left hand on his desk. "This is ridiculous. I'm going to call and tell them to cancel his transfer request."

Sunny lifted a staying hand. "No. I don't want you to interfere."

Gramps frowned unhappily. He looked around his desk until he found a roll of antacid tablets. "Why the devil not?" he demanded as he popped one into his mouth.

"Because you've done quite enough already in forcing Zach to marry me."

Gramps chased the antacid tablet with a gulp of water. "No one held a gun to his head."

"Close enough," Sunny said ruefully. "Besides, this is his decision."

"You mean that, don't you?" Gramps said.

Sunny nodded. She took a closer look at her grand-father. He seemed a little pale. "Say, are you feeling okay?"

He waved off her concern. "Too much spicy food for lunch. It was Mexican Day over at the diner. Listen, I forgot to mention it, but I'd like to go off on a fishing trip for a few days. That okay with you?"

Sunny nodded. "Of course."

"Are you sure?" Without warning, he looked a little anxious. "'Cause I could cancel it if you need me here."

"Don't be silly. You just go off and have fun. I'll hold the fort down." And wait for Zach to make a decision and retract the transfer. Sunny could only hope he would make the right decision for both of them. Their marriage had started out for all the wrong reasons, but now that they were married, they were growing closer day by day, maybe even falling in love. She wanted a chance to see their relationship through. She didn't want to look back later and think they might have had something really special if only they'd given themselves the chance.

"YOUR MAMA IS just going to kill me," Gertie told four-year-old Toby as she ushered him into the Carlisle Clinic.

Toby looked at Zach, then Gertie. "Did you swallow a marble, too?" Toby asked Gertie.

"Toby swallowed a marble?" Zach interrupted.

Gertie wrung her hands. "That's what he said. I didn't even know he had any marbles with him."

"I always keep them in my pocket, right here," Toby said importantly. He patted the front right pocket on his child-size jeans, then reached inside and pulled out a white-and-green marble. "See?" He held it up for both adults. "It was just like this one and I put it in my mouth—"

"No!" Gertie and Zach said in unison when Toby started to demonstrate how he had swallowed the first marble.

"Here, honey, let me hold that for you," Gertie said as perspiration broke out on her brow. She placed the marble in her purse.

"When did you realize he had swallowed a marble?" Zach asked, perplexed because Toby was showing none of the expected signs of respiratory distress or physical discomfort.

"When he told me, about ten minutes ago," Gertie said, looking as if she might burst into tears at any second.

"Where's Rhonda-Faye?"

"At home with the new baby, asleep. She was up all night and I told her that I would take Toby this morning while the others went to school, since it's my day off."

"That was nice of you," Zach said.

"Rhonda-Faye will not think so when she finds out what happened," Gertie said, nervously fingering the strand of pearls around her neck. "She will think I am a complete novice with kids."

"She doesn't know what happened?"

"After all she's been through with George and the baby coming early, I thought I'd better find out how bad it was, first. How bad is it?"

Zach touched Gertie's shoulder reassuringly as Toby gravitated to the box of toys and books in the far corner of the room. "There's one way to find out."

"So you'll take a quick look at him before we call Rhonda-Faye or George and tell them?" Gertie said.

Zach paused, watching as Toby tried out a child-size chair and seemed to like it. What Gertie was asking of him was highly unusual. "Normally, I need a parent's verbal or written permission to treat a child."

"What about on an emergency basis?" Gertie pressed.

"Then treatment can be rendered after getting express permission from the adult caring for the child," Zach said.

"Which is me," Gertie interrupted.

"Right."

"So what do you say?" she asked anxiously.

Zach smiled. "Under the circumstances, I think it would be permissible to find out what kind of shape Toby's in before we call his folks. There's no use upsetting them unnecessarily."

"And you know how excited George gets in any medical emergency," Gertie murmured.

Zach nodded. "We don't want him having another accident trying to make it to the clinic." One set of stitches had been enough.

Zach stepped closer to his young patient, who, unlike Gertie, was remarkably calm. "Toby, how about coming into an examining room so I can listen to your lungs?" Zach said.

Toby moved away from the box of toys in the corner of the waiting room. He had a storybook in his hand. "Can I bring this with me, Dr. Zach?"

"Sure." Zach grinned. "So how do you like your new sister?"

Toby made a face. "She cries a lot and she goes to the bathroom in her pants."

"Diapers," Zach corrected.

"Whatever," Toby said, climbing up onto the pediatric table with Zach's help. "It's disgusting. All my brothers think so."

"I bet."

"Sounds like sibling rivalry," Gertie said.

Zach nodded. He helped Toby pull off his shirt, then looked into his young patient's throat. "Say 'ahhh.'"

"Ahh."

Zach listened to Toby's chest. "Are you sure you swallowed that marble? That it didn't just fall out of your mouth—maybe on the floor somewhere?"

"I swallowed it all right. It hurt a little when it went down, too," Toby declared.

"Does it hurt now?" Zach asked.

"No. But it did then," Toby said.

Zach took another long careful look at the boy's throat. He could find no evidence that the four-year-old had swallowed anything. "If he did swallow a marble, it appears to have gone into his stomach," Zach told Gertie.

Gertie looked as if she were going to burst into tears any second. "Can't you find it?"

"Not so far, but to be on the safe side, we'll do an X ray and see if we can locate it that way," Zach told her.

"It's not there," he said, fifteen minutes later as the three of them studied the X rays.

"But how is that possible?" Gertie cried, looking all the more upset.

Zach wondered the same thing. He turned to Toby, who was looking sideways at the pictures of his insides. "Toby, when did you swallow the marble? Was it before or after Gertie picked you up?"

"Before."

"How long before?"

"I dunno." Toby shrugged his small shoulders.

"This morning?" Zach pressed.

Toby shook his head. "Last Christmas."

"Last Christmas," Zach echoed as he and Gertie shared a relieved laugh.

"Yeah." Toby appeared confused. He did not get what they were chuckling about.

"Did you tell your mom and dad you swallowed this marble?" Zach asked.

"Nope."

"Why not?"

"I dunno. I forgot, I guess. Christmas is a pretty busy time. Can I have a sticker now?" Toby asked hopefully.

"Sure." Zach got out a whole box of them from the cabinet. "You were such a good patient, you may have two."

"Okay, but can I look through all of them first before I have to pick?" he asked.

"Take your time," Zach said.

Gertie turned to Zach. "I suppose it's safe to assume the marble went the way of everything else Toby ingests but doesn't need?"

Zach nodded.

"I'm so embarrassed," Gertie said, covering her eyes with her white lace hankie.

"Been there," Zach said.

Gertie grinned at him. "I suppose you have. So, how are you enjoying married life?"

Zach hesitated. What could he say to that? He liked being with Sunny. But marriage . . . what kind of marriage was it when the vows were not taken seriously and the couple didn't even share the same bed?

"Just what I thought," Gertie said. "The two of you still have the honeymoon blues."

"Honeymoon blues?" Zach asked.

"You know. The getting-adjusted-to-everything blues. But take it from me, Zach—" Gertie patted his arm reassuringly "—I know just what the two of you need."

"NEED A RIDE?"

The low, familiar voice sent shudders of awareness down her spine. "Zach." Sunny flushed as she clasped her clipboard to her chest and turned to face him. He was wearing a blue chambray dress shirt, red tie and jeans. His hair was wind tossed and sexy, his jaw freshly shaven and scented with the after-shave she liked. "What are you doing here?"

"Enjoying the scenery." Looking relaxed and at ease, he stepped away from the entrance to the factory display room and closed the short distance between them.

Her shoulder nudging his, Sunny said, "There is no scenery in here."

He chucked her on the chin and grinned down at her. "Gotta differ with you there, babe. There's plenty of scenery in this room."

The compliment was as heartfelt as it was teasing. Response trembled along her skin. "The new display rooms are nice, aren't they?" Sunny said, being deliberately obtuse.

Zach nodded and cast an admiring glance around. The room they were standing in featured living room furniture, done in a timeless traditional style.

"Yes, it's very nice. I noticed, coming in, that the rooms are really put together down to the last detail. Having the right accessories makes the furniture look even classier."

Sunny nodded. "I know. I've been thinking the same thing. That's why I'm trying to get my grandfather to enlarge our operation here and sell accessories—like quilts and pictures and lamps. Maybe even a line of coordinating, custom-made draperies."

"Going to turn Carlisle's into the next Sears Roebuck?"

"More like an L. L. Bean Furniture store and catalog. Our look will stay pure Tennessee."

He took her hand in his and tugged her over to the red-and-green plaid sofa. "None of that eclectic postmodern stuff for you, hmm?"

Sunny made a face. "No way."

"How come?" He sat down next to her.

Sunny sat back against the cushions. "Because I love what warm, cozy furniture can do to a room— transform it from a utilitarian space to a place to regroup, and replenish the soul."

"Old-fashioned furniture for an old-fashioned girl."

"Absolutely. Does that bother you?"

"Just makes me curious. You seem so open-minded about everything else. Why not with modern furniture, too?" Zach's eyes locked on hers.

Sunny shrugged. He was seeing too much again. Zeroing in on her vulnerable side without half trying. "That's all we ever had in our home, growing up. There's something very cold about it, at least for me. And I just don't like it, so I'm not going to make it, and I'm not going to sell it."

Zach wondered if she was talking about furniture now or her parents. "Sorry. I didn't mean to upset you."

"No." Sunny shook her head and ran a hand through her hair. "I'm sorry for snapping at you. It's just been a long day."

Gertie had been right. Sunny did need some tender, loving care. Fortunately, he was just the man to give it to her, Zach thought, as he walked her out to his pickup.

Sunny stopped short when they reached the door and she looked inside. "What's all this?" she asked, pointing to the wicker picnic baskets, blankets and thermos.

"Supper. I thought maybe you'd take me up to the top of the mountain so we could enjoy the view."

"You haven't been there yet?" As she gazed up at him, her breath was uneven, shivers raced along her spine.

"No. And I've been told it's the greatest place to watch the sunset."

"It is." It was also highly romantic. For that reason alone, Sunny told herself she should not go there with him. She turned and stepped up into the truck. Aware she felt happy and sad simultaneously, she asked, "Why are you doing this?"

Zach leaned in to assist her with her seat belt. He smiled at her, his blue eyes dazzling in their intensity.

"You pampered me," he said softly, pausing to kiss her temple. "I thought it was high time I did the same for you."

One kindness begets another...wasn't that what they'd taught in her marriage class? Was it possible the theory worked, even in their case? Sunny wondered, amazed as Zach drove the short distance to their picnic site and parked the truck at the end of the old gravel logging road.

"You're awfully quiet," he said. He got out, grabbed the picnic gear and circled around to her side.

Sunny was wishing she were not nearly so susceptible to him. She was also wishing she had her tennis shoes instead of her flats. She was lucky, though, that she had on trousers instead of a dress. "I was thinking about the bid we won today," Sunny fibbed. As they spread out the blankets, she told him about it.

"The Southern Hospitality Inn is part of a big hotel chain, isn't it?" Zach asked as he brought out beef-brisket sandwiches, potato salad.

Sunny nodded. "They've got four-star hotels in practically every major city of the country."

"So this could lead to other jobs and really put Carlisle Furniture on the map," Zach said as he added zesty vinegar slaw, homemade dill pickles and an assortment of black and green olives to their plates.

Sunny poured them each generous glasses of iced tea. "We hope it leads to more work." Famished, she bit into her sandwich.

"If that happens, would you move the factory elsewhere, open a second one or expand here?"

"I think I'd try to expand here," she said cautiously. She settled in beside him, appreciating the quiet beauty of their surroundings and the intimacy of being with him. Zach had put a lot of thought into the evening, and she had needed to get away from it all, more than she had realized.

"Bringing a lot of people in would change the community."

"I know, and that worries me." Sunny set her plate aside. She brought her knees up to her chest and wrapped her arms around them. "I like living in a small town."

Zach looked out at the countryside below. Carlisle was visible in the distance, rooftops popping up between the trees on peaceful shady streets. Old-fashioned but neatly kept, the town resembled something out of a Norman Rockwell painting. And though it was beautiful, it was also dull. "You don't think you'll get bored here eventually? Carlisle is awfully small."

Sunny's jaw set stubbornly. "I need more than an intellectual challenge to keep me happy. I need the feeling of belonging and closeness, of community, that living here gives me."

"Your parents didn't feel the same way, I guess."

"No, they didn't. For all their lawyerly brilliance, they are never going to understand why I care so much about the people in this town, or why I want to take care of the business and keep it growing and thriving so the town can still exist. The employees aren't numbers to me. They're people, with faces and names and personalities and families to support. I like knowing everyone here. I like knowing that what I do is making a tremendous difference in their lives and in the overall soundness of Gramps's company."

"Taking care of people is very satisfying."

Sunny gazed into his eyes, saw the compassion there, and knew he really did understand. More so than she had expected that he would. "You're speaking as a physician."

Zach shrugged. For an instant he was moodily silent, pulling away from her. "And a member of my own family."

His brooding look gone almost as soon as it appeared, Zach lifted a forkful of potato salad to her lips. "Recognize the recipe?"

Sunny smiled. "Gertie's."

"Right." Zach fed her another forkful of potato salad. "She cooked the whole meal for us."

"That was sweet of her. I'll have to thank her."

He smiled at her warmly as she took another bite of her sandwich. "I already did, for both of us."

He was acting as if they were a real couple, she thought. Or maybe he was just getting into the swing of pretending, for as long as he was there.

The sandwich suddenly turning to sawdust in her throat, Sunny swallowed. She felt angry and hurt, and she had no right to feel either, she told herself sternly. He wasn't breaking any promises to her, because he'd never made any commitment.

Around them, the sunlight faded to a dusky romantic glow. Zach paused to light an outdoor candle in a mason jar.

"You don't mind that I agreed to let her cook for us, do you?" he said, his expression concerned.

"No, of course not," Sunny said, sitting Indianstyle again. *I mind that you are trying to leave here, and you haven't even bothered to tell me. Despite the fact that I am your wife!* Then again, she thought, he wasn't acting like a man with one foot out the door tonight. And Gramps had succeeded in blocking his transfer, at least temporarily. Thinking of Gramps, she wondered if he still had his indigestion tonight. He had left the factory early to pack for his trip, which was slated to begin that evening.

"Sunny?" Zach touched her hand. "You look... upset. Is everything okay?"

She slipped her hand in his, glad she had him to confide in. "It's Gramps," she said, swallowing around the lump in her throat. "I don't think he was feeling all that well today."

Zach grew very still. "What seemed to be the matter?"

"He was rubbing his shoulder and guzzling antacids."

Zach's eyes darkened. "Did he say he was in pain?"

"No." She lifted her face to his. Without warning, her heart was pounding. "Why would you ask that?"

"Because I'm a doctor." Zach regarded her patiently. "Those are the kinds of questions I'm supposed to ask."

"Oh." Sunny forced herself to calm down. "No, he just seemed . . . I don't know . . . generally uncomfortable, a little anxious and upset."

Zach looked down at his plate. "He's taking a few days off to go fishing, isn't he?" he said casually.

Sunny nodded, not sure why but she felt something was amiss here. "How did you know that?"

"He mentioned it to me last week."

"So you don't think I should worry?"

Zach shifted restlessly on the blanket beside her. "I don't think Augustus would go off on a three-day fishing trip if he were ill, do you?"

"No." Sunny forced herself to relax. "You're right. He wouldn't. I guess I'm just overreacting—that's all. Gramps means so much to me." Her voice caught. "He's the only one who's ever believed in me." Tears stung her eyes. "I don't know what I'd do without him."

Zach reached over to squeeze her hand. "Luck willing, he'll be with us a long time to come, but if it will make you feel any better, I'll check up on him, too."

"Thanks, Zach. I appreciate it."

"Is everything okay with you?" he continued. "You look a little stressed out tonight, too."

Sunny shook off her confusion. It was going to be dark soon, and with the stars and the moon overhead, oh, so romantic. "I'm just tired—that's all," she said. And that was true. She didn't want to talk about his transfer request or what Gramps had done to block it. She smiled at Zach encouragingly. "How was your day?"

At the mention of his work, Zach broke into a wide grin. "I saw one of Rhonda-Faye and George's little boys." He recounted the marble incident in great detail. By the time he had finished, Sunny was laughing right along with him.

"Toby is something else," she murmured sympathetically, pleased that Zach had such a sense of humor about the whole incident and that he was quickly warming to the people in the community.

Zach shook his head. "I should have asked the little tyke *when* he swallowed the marble right off."

Sunny shrugged. "Live and learn." And that could be said about everything.

They both smiled. He leaned over in the picnic basket and brought out another container. "And now for the pièce de résistance," he said with a flourish. "Double-chocolate walnut brownies."

Sunny groaned in feigned ecstasy. "My favorite."

"I can think of something I like better," Zach murmured as he started to take her in his arms.

Her heart racing, Sunny flattened a palm against his chest to keep him from coming any closer. She wanted him, and she didn't. "No, Zach. No kissing," she said breathlessly.

He fastened his eyes on hers as he teased, "Not even just one?"

She shook her head firmly, ignoring his obvious disappointment—and hers. "Not even one."

SUNNY'S LOW melodious voice floated out into the backyard as Zach headed toward the door, sack of groceries in his arms.

"Matilda's really having trouble." Sunny laughed softly, then continued speaking into the phone. "Easy for you and me, but we grew up using computers. She didn't. I think it would be a good idea if you came back and stayed until she has the hang of the entire order-entry system." She paused, head bent, listening intently. "I know it'll be expensive, but it'll be worth it." Sunny paused again, then laughed softly. "I really appreciate it, Chuck. I consider it a personal favor. Right. See you then. Looking forward to it."

Sunny hung up the phone and turned around to see Zach lounging in the kitchen doorway. From the expression on her face, he guessed she had been wondering how much he had overheard of her telephone conversation. Enough to make him damn jealous, Zach thought. Never mind that the emotion was completely irrational; it was there.

"Back already?" she asked lightly.

He nodded, trying hard not to notice how much she wanted to get rid of him this evening, or how much it stung to realize she felt that way. He carried the single bag of groceries into the kitchen and set it down on the counter, next to the fridge. "Milk, cereal and a fresh loaf of bread, just like you asked." He began putting them away. "And I also checked on Gramps—" who was now in the Knoxville hospital, undergoing tests "—and he's fine."

"Thank you," Sunny said gratefully.

Zach nodded. He just wished he could tell her everything about her grandfather.

Noting the coffee had stopped brewing, Sunny poured herself a mug. She had work papers scattered over the kitchen table. "And thanks for getting the groceries, too. Normally I wouldn't ask you to run an errand, but I have so much to do tonight. And I didn't want you to wake up to an empty refrigerator and no breakfast.''

''Sounds like those how-to-be-a-loving-wife lessons are really sinking in,'' he teased.

Sunny's jaw set rebelliously even as she studiously avoided his eyes. Zach stepped closer and took her into his arms. She splayed a hand across his chest to prevent him from coming any nearer. Hurt and wariness glimmered in her eyes.

Suddenly Zach knew he had to ask. ''What's wrong, Sunny?'' Acquiescing to her obvious wishes, he dropped his hands from her shoulders. ''You've been acting funny all evening.''

She stepped back and tossed her head. ''I'm a regular laugh riot, aren't I?'' she retorted sadly.

Zach struggled against the urge to bury his hands in the shimmering softness of her red-gold hair. He lounged against the counter, instead, bracing a hand on either side of him. ''Have I done or said something to make you uncomfortable?''

She regarded him indifferently. ''What would make you think that?''

''The fact that you wouldn't stay and watch the sunset with me at the top of Carlisle Mountain.''

Sunny shrugged. She picked up her coffee mug again and took a sip. ''The roads get dangerous after dark.''

Zach knew an excuse when he heard one. It infuriated him to see her putting up barriers between them, just when he'd begun to tear them down. ''Ten to one it never bothered you before.''

She flushed guiltily, confirming his suspicions that she was trying hard to keep them from getting any closer. "And then there is the quick way you sent me off to the store, the determined way you are immersing yourself in your work."

Sunny tightened her hands around her mug. "I have things to do tonight, Zach."

He sensed her work was nothing that couldn't wait until morning. "You're hiding something from me, Sunny."

"Because I didn't want to kiss you tonight?" she said coolly.

"That's part of it," he said slowly, knowing in his gut there was more to the sudden distrust in her eyes. If he'd done something to annoy her, he wanted to know about it.

Sunny released a troubled sigh. Confusion colored her low voice. "I don't want to play house with you, Zach."

"Is that what you think we've been doing?" *He* thought they'd been building something important here, growing closer.

Sunny raked her teeth across her lip. "I don't know what we've been doing. Or even how or why I allowed myself to get sucked into this. All I know is that our marriage is only a temporary arrangement, Zach, one we both entered into for all the wrong reasons."

He couldn't dispute that. But he thought that they'd been making progress by the way she kissed him and melted in his arms at the slightest touch, that she wanted to make love as much as he did. Apparently he'd been wrong. "Meaning what?" Zach returned, unable to keep his disappointment in check. "That our marriage is going to remain one in name only?"

"Of course." Sunny planted her hands on her hips and regarded him exasperatedly. "Why would you ever have expected anything else?"

Chapter Nine

Woman, Walk the Line

"I'm glad you're back," Zach told Gramps several days later, when he stopped by the clinic upon his return.

Augustus handed over copies of his files, sent by the Knoxville Hospital. "So am I. If I'd had to pretend to be on a fishing trip much longer, Sunny would've gotten suspicious."

Zach had already been informed of the test results by phone, but he welcomed the chance to look at the lab reports himself. "How are you feeling?"

Augustus sank into a chair. "Better than I have in weeks, though why that should be after three days of lying around in a hospital bed is a mystery, to be sure."

"The rest in between tests probably did you good."

"Made me antsy is more like it. When will I know what's causing my chest pains?" he asked, frowning anxiously.

"I'm not sure," Zach said honestly, wishing he had better news to relate. Augustus's symptoms still had them all baffled. "So far all we've managed to do is rule things out. Your heart and lungs are fine. The dentist says there's no sign you've been grinding your teeth, which is something that can also cause chest pain. And your GI series was fine. Of course, the pain you've been experiencing could still be indigestion and linked to something you're eating, a particular spice or food. It just didn't show up as inflammation or anything serious in the tests.'' And Zach was relieved about that. Whatever was going on, Augustus was not dying.

"So what next?" Augustus asked with a relieved sigh.

Zach picked up a pencil and turned it end over end. "There's got to be a pattern to these episodes. It's up to us to play medical detective and track it down. So the moment you have chest pain,'' Zach admonished seriously, "I want you to drop everything and come and see me. I don't care what time of day or night it is. We will figure this out.''

Augustus nodded. "In the meantime, is it all right if I go fishing—for real this time? I've missed my rod and reel.''

"Sure. As long as you don't overdo.''

"I won't. Sunny doesn't suspect a thing, does she?''

"No," Zach said. And he felt bad about keeping it from her. He'd wanted to confide in her the other night so much. These days, he didn't want anything between them holding them apart, not even her grandfather's secret.

"So WHAT DO you think, Doc?" Matilda said, showing Zach her red, blistered hands.

"I think you've got one of the worst cases of contact dermatitis I've ever seen. What have you been doing?"

"I've been washing dishes over at the diner and filling in for Rhonda-Faye, who's still out with her new baby."

"Well, you need to wear gloves when you put your hands in water, and apply this cream to your hands four times a day in the meantime."

"Will do. And Doc?"

"Yes, Matilda?"

"About those classes Sunny has been taking. She's really been putting her heart into them."

This was news to Zach.

"The only thing is, and I don't know quite how to say this and still be tactful."

"Just spit it out, Matilda."

"Well, judging by the reports Sunny has been giving back to the group, the other ladies and I feel that you may not be doing your part in return."

"Let me get this straight." Zach tamped down his anger with effort. "Sunny has been telling your group that I'm a bad husband?"

"Oh, no. Sunny would never say that, Doc. It's just sometimes when she's making her reports I get the feeling she's kind of disappointed in the way things have worked out. Don't get me wrong. She puts on a brave front and speaks in a cheerful tone, but underneath...well, I think in her heart she was wishing you all had had a more conventional or romantic start."

She wasn't the only one, Zach thought.

"But I think she really is trying. I think she wants this marriage of yours to work." Matilda pressed a hand to her ample bosom. "Oh, dear, I can see I've offended you with all my frank talk, haven't I?"

"It does seem like a violation of privacy, knowing what's going on in our marriage is being reported back to that class," Zach said.

"Slim doesn't like it, either," Matilda freely admitted. "And some of the lessons have given us rather confounding results. But overall he likes the changes the class is bringing to our marriage. And the same goes for all the other husbands. Why, we haven't paid this much attention to each other in years!" Matilda said. "If you would just give the class—and Sunny— a chance, Zach, I know the two of you could be happy," she said kindly.

Could they? he wondered, a little guiltily. He knew he hadn't given the relationship or Sunny a chance initially, but lately they had become a lot closer anyway. Was it possible that she was more serious than he'd been led to believe? Was it possible she wanted to make their marriage a real one, too? And that her testy behavior was due to her disappointment in him rather than her chafing at the increasingly intimate situation in which they found themselves? If that was the case, if Sunny was really trying to make this marriage of theirs work in her own convoluted way, Zach saw he owed her an apology.

"Furthermore, I know how you can make it up to her. Slim and the boys have all offered to help," Matilda continued exuberantly.

Making up with Sunny seemed like a good idea. Having the whole community in on the plan did not. "Help me how?" Zach asked warily.

"Why, help make Sunny feel better," Matilda said. "All you have to do is show up at our house, say around 9:00 p.m.?"

"YOU'RE WHERE?" Sunny gasped into the telephone. She had expected her parents to be angry with her, not rush to her side.

"About ten minutes away from your house," her mother replied. "You had to know that as soon as we received your letter we'd want to see you."

Suddenly her desire to get even with her parents for trying to dupe her into marrying Andrew did not seem like such a good idea. "You're planning to stay with Gramps, aren't you?" Sunny asked nervously.

"Honey, we want to stay with you. We want to get to know your husband and well...help you straighten things out. Oh, your father's waving at me. Gotta run."

Sunny stared at the phone. Her parents there in ten minutes? Heart pounding, she raced for the stairs. Grabbing a stack of Zach's clothes and medical journals, she tossed them about the master bedroom, then raced back to the guest room to get the rest of his stuff. Her parents mustn't guess this was a marriage in name only or she'd never hear the end of her foolhardiness. And considering the way things were turning out, Sunny thought, as she wiped a stream of perspiration from her brow, she knew they would be right.

Finished moving most of his stuff, she put a set of clean sheets on the bed in the master bedroom, hung fresh towels in the bathroom, tidied the sink and then raced for the linen closet again. She had just picked out a set of fresh sheets for the guest-room bed, when she heard it. The unmistakable sound of Slim's fiddle, Fergus's guitar, George's banjo and Gramps's harmonica! And a familiar voice singing…"Love Me Tender"?

She swore again. She didn't know what Zach was up to now, but his timing couldn't be worse.

ZACH FELT LIKE a fool standing in front of Sunny's stoop, a bunch of daisies in hand, singing love songs off-key. Worse, the racket he and the band were making was causing quite a commotion. Doors and windows were opening all over the neighborhood. Including Sunny's.

A come-hither smile on her face, she sauntered out to greet him. "Welcome home, sweetheart," she purred, lacing her arms about his neck. Standing on tiptoe, she kissed him soundly on the lips.

Telling himself the best way to end the impromptu concert was to act as if he and Sunny had much better things to do than stand out there singing all night, Zach wrapped both arms about her waist and shifted her close. Ignoring the way she stiffened in surprise, he gave the kiss all he had and then some.

Male laughter sounded behind him. Then applause.

"See, Zach?" Slim said. "Told you that serenading her with love songs would work."

"Always does," George agreed.

"I think you fellas better let me take my husband inside," Sunny crooned. "Before we really put on a show."

Zach inclined his head in Sunny's direction. "You heard the woman, fellas." He was glad he didn't have to do any more singing.

"We'll let y'all cook while the griddle's hot," Fergus said with a naughty wink. "But if you need us to come back, so Zach can do some more singing, y'all just holler."

"Will do," Sunny promised, wrapping her slender arm about Zach's waist. She rested her head against his chest.

Zach liked the feel of having her so close. They waited on the sidewalk and waved goodbye as the fellas all drove off. "Thanks for rescuing me," Zach said with a sigh of relief.

Sunny stayed where she was as yet another car drove up. "We're not rescued yet," she murmured. "Far from it. So play along with me. Mom, Dad!" she said as an elegantly dressed couple in their fifties emerged from the rented Lincoln. "I'm so glad you could come!"

"YOU DIDN'T TELL ME we were having company," Zach whispered in Sunny's ear.

"That's because I didn't know myself until ten minutes ago," she whispered back.

"So this is your husband," Sunny's dad said, giving Zach the once-over as Sunny moved out of Zach's arm and into his.

Zach immediately snapped to attention, while Sunny hugged her folks.

"Sir." He shook hands with her father. Somehow meeting Sunny's folks made their marriage all the more real. He nodded at her mother, not sure what was expected of him, only knowing he wanted things to go smoothly for Sunny's sake. "Mrs. Carlisle."

"Please, Zach. Call us Elanore and Eli."

"You should have let us know you were coming," Sunny said as they started up the steps.

Zach had never seen Sunny's cheeks so pink, her eyes so vulnerable. He wanted to wrap her in his arms and hold her close, reassure her everything was going to be all right.

"How about some coffee?" Sunny said the minute they got in the door.

"Actually, sweetheart, we'd like to talk with you alone, if you don't mind," Eli said.

Zach excused himself. Sunny sat down on the living room sofa. "What is it?"

"You married him to get even with us, didn't you?" her father said.

"It would serve you right if I had," Sunny retorted, folding her arms in front of her. "I still can't believe you actually sent Andrew Singleton here!"

"Andrew's a nice man," Elanore said.

"Oh, please! He wanted a merger, not a marriage!" Sunny shouted back. "And to think I almost fell for it."

"What happened?" Zach appeared in the doorway, a grim look on his face. Sunny could tell he'd heard everything.

"Zach, this is none of your concern," Elanore said.

"He's my husband. Of course it's his concern," Sunny interrupted, motioning Zach into the living room. "My parents set me up with the son of a fellow attorney shortly after I moved here. He pretended to be vacationing. He was really sent here on a mission to sweep me off my feet and get me out of Carlisle permanently. It would have worked if I hadn't figured out the connection as we started to make our wedding plans."

"Sunny confronted Andrew about the situation," Elanore continued. "And the wedding was off. She's still angry with us, which is why, no doubt, she did not let us know about your wedding in time for us to attend."

Sunny thrust out her chin stubbornly. "I didn't want you to try to stop it."

"You're saying it should have been stopped?" Eli retorted.

"Eli, dear, we did not come here to fight with Sunny. We came here to make up with her and lend whatever assistance she needs." Elanore cast a glance at Zach, who was hovering protectively at Sunny's side. "Perhaps she doesn't need as much help as we thought. At any rate, this is probably something best talked out in the morning."

Eli sighed. "I guess you're right. We have been on our feet for twenty-two hours straight now."

They did look exhausted, Sunny noted. Maybe they cared about her more than she'd thought. "I've already made up your room. You can have ours," she said.

Her parents said good-night and went quietly up the stairs. Zach waited until he heard the bedroom door shut, then took her by the hand and led her out onto the front porch. "Did you marry me to get back at them?" he asked grimly.

"It started out that way." Sunny swallowed, knowing she owed him honesty and a lot more. "But now it's turned into so much more than that, Zach. And furthermore,'' she said, her heart beating wildly, ''I don't care what my parents think about my marrying you the way I did. They are not going to interfere in my relationship with you and that's final!''

Zach realized Sunny was offering him what he had always wanted in a relationship. ''I'm glad to hear that,'' he said with a grin, ''because those are my sentiments exactly.''

''YOU DIDN'T TELL them the truth about our marriage, did you?'' Zach asked as he and Sunny made up the bed in the guest room.

Sunny paused to look at Zach. For a person who hated familial interference, he was taking this all remarkably well. ''They already think my moving to Tennessee was a mistake.''

''How come?''

Sunny poured her heart out to him. ''Because in their opinion, there's nothing for me here.'' She plumped a pillow almost violently. ''They saw I had the very best education. Now they want me to put it to better use,'' she confided bitterly, as she plopped down on the edge of the half-made bed.

Zach sat down beside her. He wrapped a comforting arm around her shoulders and pulled her close. ''They don't know you at all, do they?'' he commiserated softly.

Sunny rested her face on his shoulder. She loved the way he felt, so warm and solid and strong. ''They never have,'' she admitted sadly. ''I used to think it was my fault, but now I know that's not true. They love me in their own way. But it's in a detached way one moment, a smothering way the next. There's never any happy medium with them."

He held her closer. "I'm sorry." He rubbed her arm consolingly and turned toward her.

"Why?" Loving their intimacy, Sunny buried her face in the curve of his neck.

"Because living that way has obviously been very tough on you."

Sunny luxuriated in the brisk wintry scent that was him, then drew back to look at him seriously. "Are you close to your folks?" she asked quietly at length, wondering if he'd had a happier childhood than she had.

Zach nodded, all too willing to admit it as he squeezed her hand in his. "I can tell them just about everything."

The edges of her lips began to curl. "Except that we're married," she said, taking a guess.

Zach nodded. He looked deep into her eyes. "But only because they'd worry about me if they knew it wasn't a real marriage, and they'd want to celebrate with me if they thought it was. I felt we already had enough interference in our lives as it was."

Sunny breathed a shaky sigh of relief. "I'll second that," she said with a light laugh. She didn't know what she would do if they had another set of parents on their doorstep.

Turning slightly toward him, so their knees were touching, Sunny rested the palm of her hand just above his knee. "Do you have any brothers and sisters?"

"It's just me, my mom and dad now," Zach said, a brooding look appearing suddenly on his face. "I had a sister who died," he said quietly after a moment.

But to Sunny's increasing disappointment, he didn't continue. He climbed in on his side of the bed, turned his back to her and shut his eyes. Seconds later, he was asleep.

Sunny lay staring at the ceiling, thinking of all the kisses they'd shared, and the ones they hadn't. So much for her worrying about her virtue, she thought. Even in the same bed, married to the man, she couldn't have been safer. It was turning out to be exactly what she wanted, a night that was affable enough to fool her parents into thinking everything was fine between her and Zach. So why was she feeling so disappointed?

ZACK AWOKE at the first light of dawn to find a stack of pillows and a rolled-up blanket between Sunny and him. He eased from the bed, grabbed a robe and headed downstairs. He wouldn't be able to dress for work until he could get to his clothes, which Sunny had stuffed in her closet. And he wouldn't be able to do that until her parents were awake.

To his surprise, Eli and Elanore were already in the kitchen. They had made a pot of coffee and were working on a thick stack of legal papers.

"We're still on European time," Elanore explained.

Zach nodded. "I saw the packed suitcases in the front hall," he said. He wondered how Sunny would react to that.

"We've got a meeting in New York late this afternoon," Eli explained. "We're flying out of Memphis-Nashville at 1:00 p.m."

Which meant they would have to leave in a few hours, Zach thought. Sunny was going to be so disappointed.

"So where did you go to med school, Zach?" Eli asked.

"Vanderbilt," he said, knowing the third degree had a purpose. They wanted to know if he was good enough for their daughter.

Eli and Elanore beamed their approval at his alma mater.

"Good school. Very prestigious," Eli said.

"So how did you end up here?" Elanore asked.

Zach resented the implication that Carlisle was somehow less important because it was a rural location. "I had a contract with the state. They paid my tuition. In turn, I promised two years of service in a rural area."

"Of your choice?"

"Actually, it was a little more complicated than that. I applied to a number of places and then was assigned," Zach said. Which reminded him, he should check and see how his transfer request was going. Not that he was so inclined to leave now that he was beginning to get settled in at the clinic and he and Sunny had declared a truce. In fact, were things to progress to the point where he and Sunny became lovers he wasn't sure he would want to leave at all. Until his two-year assignment in Carlisle was up, of course.

"Well, Sunny had an excellent education, too," Elanore said.

"Her mother and I really think she is going through a phase and that she'll live up to her potential as soon as she gets this sojourn here out of her system," Eli said. "It probably had something to do with all those sociology classes she took at Smith."

"My being here has nothing to do with all the classes I took at college," Sunny said angrily. She stormed into the kitchen, hair in disarray, her terry-cloth robe wrapped tightly around her waist. "Furthermore, I resent your telling Zach that is the case."

"Now, Sunny," Elanore said with a beleaguered sigh. "It's not that we want to fight with you."

Sunny spread her hands. Her eyes sparkled with tears. "Then why did you come here? Why are you saying all these things?"

"Because we feel you're wasting your potential here," Eli explained gently. "With your education and credentials, you could be working for a top Fortune 500 company."

"I'm a CEO here," Sunny stressed.

"Of a regional furniture company, honey!" Eli shot back.

To Zach's surprise, Sunny kept quiet about her plans to expand Carlisle Furniture with a mail-order catalog business.

She folded her arms in front of her. "Why don't you just say it?" she retorted thickly. "The fact that I've come back here to live and work is embarrassing you in front of all your colleagues and friends."

"It's just that you're capable of so much more," Elanore said gently.

Eli nodded in affirmation. "We've got friends in influential places. We could call in a few markers and get you a job on the fast track, in Europe or here in the States.''

Sunny swept a hand through her hair. Her mouth tightened. She stared at her parents in exasperation, then looked at Zach.

He knew she needed him. ''I think Sunny is happy right where she is,'' he said firmly, moving to stand beside his wife and lace an arm about her shoulders. ''And as far as I'm concerned, that's all that matters.''

''THANKS FOR helping out like that,'' Sunny said after her parents had left, and they were both upstairs getting ready to go to work. ''Though given the way you feel about living in Carlisle yourself, I'm not sure why you did.''

''You've got to make your own decisions, Sunny. Although their remarks did leave me with a few questions of my own.''

''Such as?''

She plugged in her curling iron and sat down at the vanity table next to the bathroom sink. She was dressed in a mint green shirtdress with a cinched-in waist and a long swirling skirt. She looked beautiful in a hands-off sort of way...and was also highly emotional. So much so, in fact, that Zach wished he could take the day off work and spend it just being with her, offering her what comfort he could.

''Have you ever had any second thoughts about settling here permanently?'' he asked as he smoothed shaving cream on his face.

''Let me guess,'' Sunny said grimly as she began to brush her hair. ''You think I'm wasting my time, too.''

Zach began to shave with long, smooth strokes. He hadn't agreed with Elanore and Eli's approach, but he knew they did have some valid points that should be considered. "You are well educated, with a lot of business savvy. Your parents are right. There probably are a lot of other opportunities out there for you."

Sunny leaned toward the mirror as she curled her bangs. "Living in Carlisle is like being part of one big family, and I adore it." Finished, she set her curling iron down and swiveled toward him. "Maybe if I hadn't already lived in Europe I'd want to see more of the world. But thanks to my parents, I've already seen and done so much. Right now what I want is a home, pure and simple, and I've got that here."

Zach rinsed and towel-dried his face. "Carlisle is a friendly town—I'll give you that. Everyone cares about everyone else."

"But—?"

Zach shrugged as he reached for his dress shirt and slipped it on. "I don't like having to fight for control of my own life."

Sunny raised a lecturing finger his way. "If your life is out of control, it is not because you're living in Carlisle, Zach."

He reached for his tie and put it around his neck. "Then what is it?"

Sunny brushed past him in a drift of cinnamon-scented perfume.

"Maybe the close quarters and intense public scrutiny have just forced you to really examine your life for the first time. Maybe you're uncomfortable because you don't like what you find."

Zach followed her into her bedroom. He watched as she tossed shoes out of her closet, finally settling on a pair of ivory flats. "Hey, I've got nothing to feel ashamed about. I'm working in a noble profession. I've devoted my life to caring for other people."

"But what about your private life, Zach?" Sunny asked as she slipped on her shoes. "Take it from me, there's got to be more than meaningful work to make you happy. You've got to have a personal life, too."

Zach steadied her with a hand on her waist. "That's kind of hard to do when I'm married to a woman who barely gives me the time of day." He touched a gentle hand to the side of her face. "Unless, of course, that is going to change, and we're going to have some sort of private life together?"

Sunny extricated herself from his light, possessive hold and stepped aside. Her shoulders were stiff as she turned away from him. "You knew what the terms of this arrangement were going to be when we got together, Zach."

Yes, he had. He just hadn't realized it was going to be so hard living with her and not loving her. He wondered if she was feeling as deprived of intimacy and affection as he was. "Unless you're prepared to renegotiate our agreement—" he countered hopefully.

Her eyes lit up like firecrackers. "If you're talking about sex—" Sunny warned.

Zach grabbed his billfold off the bureau and slid it in his back pocket. He figured, as long as they were laying everything on the line, they might as well be honest and up-front about this, too. "What else?"

Love, Sunny thought. *I want love. I won't settle for anything else.* "Well," she said with an arch expression, "there's cooking and cleaning—"

"Forget that," Zach grumbled. That sounded like another have-to lesson from her class on marriage.

Sunny gave him a chastising look. He wanted to make her his, all right, she mused, but only in a physical sense. "That's what I thought," she stated grimly.

"What?" Zach followed her out the bedroom and down the stairs.

She picked up a pair of gold earrings on a downstairs hall table and clipped them on her ears. "You're not interested in an equal-opportunity marriage." Her jaw set in silent censure.

Zach lounged against the banister, watching Sunny. He wasn't pleased to be sparring with her this morning. He'd much rather spend his time loving her. But at least their latest battle of the sexes had gotten her mind off her parents.

It had also brought excited color to her cheeks and a sparkle to her eyes. "Of course, I might be interested in a more chore-equitable arrangement," he teased, unable to help himself from provoking her a little more. "Providing the price was right."

Sunny shot him a look meant to cool his jets. "For instance?"

"I can see us doing the dishes together if we cozied up afterward."

Sunny knew he could. Worse, she thought, she could imagine cuddling with Zach, too. But the easy, vivid images that came to mind would not keep her heart from being broken. Only she could do that. Slowing her pulse with effort, she looked at her watch.

"I've got to get going. Matilda's waiting to give me a lift to work."

"What time do you think you'll be home tonight?" he asked. Maybe the two of them could drive down the mountain, go out to dinner...

"I don't know." Sunny frowned. "I've got a full day ahead of me, plus a supper-hour meeting with the catalog photographer and a marriage class after that. And I want to stop by and see Gramps this evening and catch him up on what's been happening at the factory since he got back from his fishing trip."

Zach shifted uncomfortably. Sunny was going to be furious when she found out where Augustus had really been.

"Don't look so upset," she scolded, misinterpreting the reason behind his dismay. "I really do have a lot to do."

Zach didn't doubt that. He also knew it wasn't his imagination. She was avoiding him like the plague. "You'll be home late, then?" he said grimly. And wondered what the men in the community would advise him to do about that. Put his foot down or weather the storm?

Sunny nodded, her expression brisk and businesslike as she picked up her briefcase. "Don't wait dinner for me."

ZACH SLID his TV dinner in the oven as the front door slammed with hurricane force. Seconds later, Sunny was framed in the kitchen doorway.

"How could you not have told me my grandfather was just hospitalized!" she stormed.

Zach swore. "How'd you find out?"

"The hospital. They called Personnel because there was a question about his insurance."

"Have you talked to him?"

"He's out fishing!"

Zach steered her resisting body into a chair. "Sit down and I'll explain." Minutes later, when he'd finished, she stared at him, looking even more upset.

"And there's still no diagnosis?" she asked, her lower lip trembling.

"No. There isn't. But we're working on it and I'm sure—" Zach's eyes tracked the sound of a car in the driveway. He looked out the window, to see a black Cadillac in the drive. Augustus got out of the car, winced as he moved toward the house. Sunny and Zach were outside in a flash. Together they helped him into the house.

"When did it start?" Zach asked. It was obvious Augustus was in pain.

"While I was fishing."

"Tell me exactly what you were doing," Zach ordered.

"Nothing to tell." He demonstrated with his left hand. "I was casting my line in the stream—" Augustus winced as he moved his arm above his head. "Damn, there it goes again."

And suddenly Zach knew what it was.

"Bursitis!" Augustus said minutes later when Zach had finished his exam and had injected steroid medication and local anesthetic into the painful joint. Together he and Sunny packed Augustus's shoulder in ice.

"All that fly-fishing you've been doing since you semiretired has aggravated your shoulder joint. The pain you felt originated there, then spread out into your chest and down your arm, mimicking heart pains or angina," Zach said. "We didn't pinpoint the source because up until now there's been no swelling or inflammation in the joint."

"But it's there now," Augustus said.

"Yes. Very visible, too. Which means you are going to have to lay off the fishing for a couple of weeks, until you heal."

"Okay," Augustus said. He blew out a weary breath. "Thanks, Zach."

"You're welcome," Zach said with a smile. He felt as relieved as Augustus looked. Sunny was not nearly as happy. She let him have it after they saw her grandfather home.

"I can't believe you kept that from me," she said tersely, marching back to Zach's truck, her hands balled into fists at her side.

"I had no choice." He walked along beside her, his shoes crunching on the gravel drive. "Augustus was my patient. And he did not want you to know."

"But what if something had happened? What if he'd been in the hospital and—" Sunny whirled to face him at the truck door. "You still should have told me. Dropped a hint. Something! I'm your wife!" Her voice was choked as she regarded him tearfully. "I thought we were close," she whispered.

"We are," Zach insisted, aware that she looked more hurt and confused than he had ever seen her.

But she only shook her head at him in a way that let him know she was comparing his machinations with Augustus to those of her parents. They had deliberately conspired to keep her in the dark.

"Not close enough, apparently," she said grimly.

His own frustration and disappointment boiling over, Zach studied her upturned face. As he had feared, Augustus's secret had driven a wedge between them. It was going to be a while before Sunny forgave him. If she did at all.

"YOU RENTED a what for us?" Zach asked Friday afternoon, when he arrived home to find Sunny lugging a suitcase down from the attic.

"I rented a houseboat for the weekend," she explained patiently, avoiding his eyes all the while.

Had she done this because she wanted to be close to him, Zach would've been exultant. But it was all too clear from the determined expression on her face that this was not the case. She was still as confused as ever, wanting to trust him, not quite sure she should. But that was something, Zach assured himself firmly, that could be overcome.

"Let me guess what prompted this," he said dryly, giving her a hand with the suitcase. "Your class, right?"

Sunny popped the case open and began filling it with clothing. "My assignment was to plan something special for just the two of us," she admitted sheepishly, pausing to look up into his face. He could tell, even if she wasn't quite ready to admit it yet, that she wanted to make up with him, too.

She wet her lips and continued softly, still holding his eyes, "I remembered what you said once about going away for the weekend being your salvation in med school and thought it might be nice to try it. That is . . . if you don't mind."

"I don't mind," Zach said, already anticipating their time alone, away from the prying eyes of the community. This was his chance to make amends with her.

As he pictured Sunny in a bikini, sunbathing on the deck of the boat, it was all he could do not to groan. The close quarters were going to be murder, just as not making love to her was going to be sheer torture. But he was looking forward to spending time with her alone, he realized, as he began to pack, also. And he could no longer deny that he did not want this marriage of theirs to end.

Chapter Ten

This Can't Be Love

"Maybe we should turn back," Sunny suggested, peering at the gray sky overhead.

"After we drove two hours to get here?" Zach said, striding down the dock. He tossed their suitcases onto the deck of their rented houseboat, then returned for the cooler full of ice and soft drinks. "Not on your life, Sunny."

She grabbed a sack of groceries from the front seat of his pickup. "What if it rains?" She didn't know why, but suddenly she was very nervous about spending the entire weekend alone with Zach. Maybe because he looked so incredibly sexy and at home on the shores of the Tennessee lake.

Zach swaggered back to her side, happier than he had been in weeks. He grabbed the last two sacks of groceries, a portable stereo and a first-aid kit. "Then we'll throw out our fishing lines and stay inside the boat."

"I don't know." Sunny continued to drag her feet. What if she found herself succumbing to the heat and passion of his kisses? A lot could happen in forty-eight hours.

Zach dumped the rest of the stuff on the deck, then turned and put his hands on her shoulders. He gazed down at her warmly. "Sunny, trust me. Everything is going to be fine. A little rain never hurt anything. Besides, the forecast calls for bright and sunny skies tonight and tomorrow. We're going to be fine."

He was right. She was being silly. "If it rains I'll just work on the catalog."

Zach lifted his brow, suddenly a lot less happy. "You brought work with you?"

"In my suitcase," Sunny confirmed. Her work had sustained her on more than one occasion. This would be no exception, she told herself firmly.

"Gonna tell your class that when you get back?" Zach teased as he gave her a hand onto the deck of the houseboat.

Sunny blushed. She could imagine the lectures she would get if she did. "That'll have to be our little secret, Zach."

"I don't know, Sunny," he drawled, rubbing his jaw.

He gave her a temptation-laced glance that set her heart to pounding.

"I'm not very good at keeping secrets."

Nor was he any good at hiding his growing desire for her, Sunny thought. "Well, try," she advised airily, aggravated to find she was blushing all the harder. Zach was acting as if this trip were going to be the honeymoon they'd never had. And damned if his feelings weren't just a bit contagious.

She had to stop thinking like this. Had to get busy.

"I'll put the galley in order," Sunny said with an outward calm she couldn't begin to feel. Aware of Zach's eyes on her, lovingly tracing every inch of her, she grabbed the groceries and slipped inside the houseboat.

Out on deck, Zach leaned over the bow of the thirty-two-foot boat and brought up anchor. Seconds later, they were on their way.

By the time they had reached the middle of the lake, the clouds had rolled in. Thirty minutes later, it began to sprinkle. Two hours later, fat raindrops thudded on the deck and roof of the houseboat.

Sunny groaned. She should have known the weather would work against them. She should have listened to the regional forecast before she'd left. Now it was too late. They were here and would just have to muddle through as best they could.

That, too, became more of a test than she'd expected as visibility soon dropped to ten feet. Swearing at the treacherous conditions, Zach steered the boat over to a secluded cove surrounded by a thick forest of trees and a steep, rocky shore. He cut the motor, then turned to face her.

"Don't suppose you located a rain slicker or umbrella anywhere in the cabin?" he asked languidly.

Sunny shook her head, aware he was going to have to leave the cabin and go out on deck to secure the boat. "Sorry."

"No problem," he said.

Sunny watched him stride out into the pouring rain. He moved around the rear of the boat. By the time he had dropped anchor and come back inside the cabin, his shirt and shorts were soaked clear through to the skin.

Sunny handed him a towel.

"Thanks," he said.

Mouth dry, she watched as he stripped off his shirt and headed into the bedroom to change. He came back out in shorts and a polo shirt, his hair slicked back from his face.

Rain pounded overhead, so loudly they had to shout to be heard. "The storm'll pass soon," Zach promised, as Sunny handed him a cup of coffee.

But the rain didn't stop. And that was when the real trouble began.

LIGHTNING SHIMMERED above, followed by a nearly simultaneous crack of thunder. Four o'clock in the afternoon, and the sky was nearly pitch-black. It was getting very scary, Sunny thought nervously as she peered out the windows for the thousandth time. In fact, it looked like tornado weather.

She paced back and forth in the small interior of the cabin, the galley on one side of her, the booth where Zach lounged on the other. Great gusts of wind rocked the boat, while rain still pounded on the roof overhead.

"You're not supposed to be in water during a thunderstorm," Sunny said shakily.

"We're not in the water. We're in a boat."

"A boat that's on water," Sunny said pointedly, wringing her hands in front of her.

"Please relax, will you?" Zach said as another jagged fork of lightning exploded in the sky. He stood impatiently. "It's just a storm. It'll be over soon."

"Just a storm," she muttered, covering her ears as another crack of tremendous thunder sounded overhead and another gust of wind shook the boat. Up above them on the bluff, lightning sliced into a towering walnut tree. A flash of fire followed, then the branch went tumbling down into the water ten feet from the bow of the houseboat. Above them, the trunk continued to smoke. The only thing that saved it from leaping into flames was the continuous downpour of rain.

Sunny shook her head, trembling over the close call. "Okay, that does it. I'm getting us out of here." She went to the captain's wheel and reached for the key in the boat ignition.

Zach was by her side in an instant. "What the hell do you think you're doing?"

"Getting us out of here." She started the boat with a roar.

He covered her hand with his and just as decisively turned the motor off. "I dropped anchor, remember?"

Fuming, Sunny whirled on him. "Then pull it up," she ordered anxiously. They were going to die out there and it was going to be all his fault.

"We're safe here in this cove," Zach said.

His implacable certainty infuriated her even more. "The only way we'll be safe is if we're back on land. Now, are you going to pull up that anchor or not?" she asked, frustrated beyond belief.

"Not." Zach took the key from the ignition, pocketed it and sat down grimly.

"Fine." Sunny leapt off the captain's seat. Her mind made up, she headed for the sliding-glass door at the front of the boat, which led out to the covered deck. He might be fool enough to want to die on this stupid boat, but that did not mean she had to join him.

Zach vaulted after her. "Come back here!" he shouted.

Sunny was already struggling around the side of the boat. The wind blew her back. She landed in Zach's arms. He clamped his arms around her decisively. "Come back inside, Sunny!" he ordered.

Bristling at the cool decisiveness in his voice, she pushed against his chest. "No!"

"You're hysterical," he shouted in her ear, holding her all the firmer.

"No, I am not, but I will be screaming if you don't let me get us out of here!" she shouted back.

Again he refused to let her go, merely turned her around so she was facing him. Arms locked around her middle like a vise, he commanded, "Stop fighting me and come back into the cabin!"

It wasn't only Zach she was fighting. It was the idea of them being alone, the thought that something terrible might happen now, this very afternoon, and her life would be all over, and she would never have known. She had to get out of there. Pulse pounding, she twisted in his arms. Swearing at her lack of cooperativeness, Zach held her all the tighter and dragged her toward the door, regardless of her feelings. The next thing she knew, she and Zach landed in a heap on the wet deck.

Still, rain pounded them, the wind roared. In the distance, Sunny saw what she had feared. The tail end of a funnel cloud touching down on the opposite side of the lake. "Oh, God, Zach!" Shaking, she pointed in the opposite direction.

His arms tightened protectively around her as he saw the tornado, too. In terrified silence, they watched it head across the lake, in a path parallel to them.

"Let's go into the cabin now," Zach said. He helped her up from the deck. They scrambled inside, both of them soaked to the skin.

The tornado continued on across the lake, touching down occasionally, sending debris flying in its wake. Finally it passed out of sight. The storm quieted somewhat. Sunny stared at the horizon for long minutes afterward, still shaking badly. "Now can we get out of here?" she said, distressed tears filling her eyes.

Zach looked at the storm around them. "I know it's bad, Sunny. I'm sorry. But we're still safer where we are," he said.

Sunny pushed the damp hair off her face. "What if another tornado comes?"

"We're still better off here than out on the lake," Zach said. He narrowed his eyes at her. "I don't suppose you brought any liquor with you?"

She shook her head mutely.

"Then we'll just have to use what we've got to calm you down," Zach said. Before she had time to resist, he scooped her up in his arms and carried her back to the bedroom...and the queen-size pull-down bed. He set her down next to it. "You're still shaking," he said, already rummaging through the clothes she'd hung up in the tiny closet. "You need to get out of those wet clothes."

"So do you." Sunny winced as lightning illuminated the curtained windows and thunder flashed overhead. But she noted the rain pounding against the windows was finally abating, the wind dying down, just a little.

He tossed her a robe and slipped out of the bedroom with his in hand. When he returned seconds later, her shorts and top were draped over the closet door to dry and she was wrapped in white terry cloth from neck to ankle. Zach was wearing a brown velour monk's robe.

"I wish the storm would end," she said miserably, glancing anxiously out the window one more time.

"So do I." Zach took her hand and led her toward the bed, while lightning flashed outside. "But since we have no control over that, we'll just have to talk until it ends."

His manner resolute, Zach guided her down and stretched out beside her. Lying back on the pillows, he dragged her wordlessly into his arms and held her close.

Sunny figured if she was going to die, she might as well go happy.

"Now, tell me," he said as he stroked his hand through her hair, "why are you so afraid of storms?"

Sunny buried her head in his chest. She felt safer with his arms around her, as though nothing could hurt her, not as long as he was there. "It goes back to the summer I was five," she said in a muffled voice, clinging to his warmth and strength. She closed her eyes, trying to relax. "We were living in Greece."

"Sounds exciting," Zach said, now stroking her hair with the flat of his hand.

"Not really," she murmured, recalling that for her the time had been anything but that. "My parents were working on an important international merger, and we were living in a villa along the coast."

"Big or little?"

"Huge. Old. Scary. Anyway, they hired this governess to take care of me. She seemed ancient at the time, but looking back, I think maybe she was only middle-aged."

"Not very nice, I guess?"

"She could put on the charm for my parents."

"But not for you?" Zach asked sympathetically.

Sunny nodded. Getting caught up in the past, she paid less and less attention to the storm outside. "Mrs. Miniver didn't believe in coddling children, and I was a kid who needed a lot of attention."

"Because you spent so much time away from your parents?" Zach said, taking a guess.

"Yes. So one night when a really bad storm blew in off the sea, Mrs. Miniver decided I needed to learn to handle my fear of thunder and lightning. So she put me in my bedroom upstairs, turned out all the lights on the floor and went back downstairs." Sunny shook her head in abject misery, remembering. "The storm went on forever, and I cried and cried. When my parents got home around two in the morning, they found me under the bed. She got fired, of course. But my fear of storms has remained. I know it's irrational, but I really hate them." Sunny shuddered, clinging to Zach all the harder as he wrapped his arms around her tightly. "I can't stand feeling as if my life might be blown apart at any minute. I can't stand not feeling safe."

"I know what you mean," he said, stroking her hair. "Safety is important to me, too," he said softly. There was a heartbeat of silence. "There's nothing worse than seeing someone you love hurting and not being able to do anything to change it," he said softly.

"You talk as if you've been in a similar situation," she said.

Zach nodded, his expression grave. "When we found out my sister, Lori, was terminal, I tried to be there for her as much as I could. It was still one of the worst times in my entire life," he said thickly. "When she died, I made a vow to myself that I would never feel that helpless again. And as you can see," he remarked with dark humor, exerting incredible self-control over his emotions, as another rumble of thunder sounded overhead, "I haven't made much, if any, progress on that score. But what the hell," he concluded with a rueful shrug and a bittersweet smile, "I'm trying my best to control the universe."

"I've noticed," she said dryly.

"Yep, I bet you have," he drawled back.

Silence fell between them once more. He grinned at her. Sunny met his smile with one of her own. It was important to her that he had confided in her. It meant a lot to be able to confide in him.

His gaze turned gentle. He traced the curve of her mouth with his fingertip, the fragile caress heating her blood.

"Feeling better?" he asked softly.

Yes and no, Sunny thought. She wanted to make love with him so badly she ached. The edges of reality and fantasy were blurring. She was beginning to feel really married to Zach, committed to him, even though she knew that was not the case. And until it was, maybe it would be better if she put some distance between them.

"You don't seem as frightened as you were," Zach continued.

The truth was, when she was in his arms, she wasn't scared at all, Sunny realized. The problem came in how she would feel when he was gone. If he left. She was still working on somehow inducing him to say.

"You know, I am feeling better, now that the worst of the storm seems to be past us," she admitted on a ragged breath, aware that wise or not, it wouldn't take much convincing at all to get her to surrender everything to him. "In fact, I think I can get up now," she said briskly, deciding the inevitable could be postponed for just a little while longer.

"Not yet," he murmured gently, rolling so she was beneath him, framing her face with his hands. He looked down at her, his eyes glowing with love. "Not until I tell you how I feel." His voice caught. "If something had happened just now, Sunny. If that tornado had hit us. If I'd lost you—"

"I know, Zach, I know. I felt the same." She held on to the edge of his robe, the raw vulnerability in his face giving her the courage to say what was in her heart, had been there all along. "But we are here. And we're together and safe."

In that instant, the world fell away, and it was just the two of them. She knew, more than anything, what she wanted. The love and closeness that had always eluded her, the desire only Zach could give.

Eyes darkening, he lowered his mouth to hers. His tongue parted her lips and swept inside her mouth. With a moan, she wreathed her arms around his neck and clasped him to her and felt his body and hers heat instantly in response.

In a haze, she let him open her robe. His hands skimmed her breasts, sensitizing the curves, until she thought she might die from the pleasure of it. Needing, wanting, more intimate contact, Sunny arched into his touch. She trembled beneath his questing fingertips, caught up in the intensity of what she was feeling, all they had become to each other and all they could be, if only they took that giant leap of faith and made their marriage a real one.

"Oh, Sunny, I want so much to make you mine." He caressed the side of her face with his thumb. "I want so much to stop thinking and just feel ... to stop planning so damn much and take a chance."

She knew exactly what he meant. "So do I, Zach." Her arms about his neck, she fitted her mouth to his and kissed him deeply, tenderly. She didn't know what the rest of her life held. And right now, selfish or not, she didn't care. She knew only that she had the chance to have a wild, reckless, incredibly passionate love affair. The chance to be with Zach like this might never come again. If she didn't take advantage of it, she would regret not making love with him the rest of her life. And she didn't want any regrets where he was concerned. She wanted only love and sweet, wonderful memories.

"Sunny, are you sure?" Zach asked, as his hands skimmed lower, slipping between her thighs. He touched her intimately, the heat of his caress sending her arching up into his questing hand.

"Yes, Zach, I'm sure," she said huskily, knowing if they weren't together now she would die.

Zach looked down into her eyes. He caressed her face lovingly, first with his eyes, then his fingertips and finally his lips. "Then I'm going to show you what love really is," he said softly, already working the robe from her shoulders, shrugging off his.

The light in the cabin was dim, but Sunny could see the beauty of his masculine shape. He was hard all over and lower still, below the waist, aroused beyond belief. Her heart pounding, the need in her an incessant ache, she closed her eyes, afraid she would lose her nerve if she thought about the enormity of the situation too much. She gripped his shoulders and took a deep breath. "All right if I let you lead the way?" she asked tremulously, never needing or wanting him more than she did at that moment, knowing what was at stake.

Zach sifted his fingers through her hair, his expression fierce with longing and the primal need to possess. Cupping her head in his hands, he angled her chin up to his. "I wouldn't have it any other way," he whispered, lowering his mouth to hers again.

His kisses melted one into another. She returned them passionately, her body feeling as if it were on fire from the inside out. She arched against his hands, yearning fervently. Sensations hammered at her. She strained against him, her body moving in undulations. "Now," she said softly, clutching at his shoulders. She was only sure she couldn't bear any more of this. She had to find a way to reach fulfillment. She had to find a way to be closer to him.

"Sunny—" He spoke as if in a haze, the hot, heavy fullness of him straining against her closed thighs.

"I want you, Zach." She slipped her hands around his hips and guided him lower still, so he was positioned precisely where he should be. She was trembling with a fierce, unquenchable ache. "I want you so much." More than she could ever have imagined. "Please. Now."

"I want you, too." He turned the words against her lips. Then he was pushing her thighs apart with his knees, stroking her gently. Sunny arched again, his name tumbling from her lips as he surged against her, penetrating the final barrier. Eyes full of wonder and fierce possessiveness, he stared down at her...and knew what she hadn't told him. "Oh, God. Sunny—" he breathed.

"Just love me, Zach," she whispered, bringing his mouth back to hers for another slow, searing, sensual kiss. "Just love me," she said again. And love her he did. His hands touched every inch of her, until she was weak with longing, overwhelmed with sensation. She surged up against him, every inch of her wanting every part of him.

ZACH LAY on his back, Sunny sprawled against his chest, her head on his shoulder. Outside, the storm had abated. Inside, as he wrapped his arms around Sunny and held her close, the storm was just beginning. In retrospect, he could see the signs had been there all along. He just hadn't wanted to deal with them because he had wanted her so much. Not just as a lover. But as his wife. "Why didn't you tell me?" he asked, stroking his hand over her slender shoulders.

Sunny snuggled against him contentedly. "Because it wasn't important." Her voice was muffled against his chest.

Like hell it wasn't. Zach was surprised by the fierce possessiveness welling inside him. He wanted only the best for Sunny. What had just happened did not fall into that category.

"Besides, I know how gallant you are at heart. You've demonstrated it many times. If I had, you would've—" She stopped, as if abruptly deciding she'd revealed too much.

Needing to see her face, he rolled so that she was beneath him. He cupped her shoulders warmly as his gaze roved her flushed features and kiss-swollen lips. "You're right, Sunny. I never would have made love to you if I'd guessed—"

She traced idle patterns on his chest. "That I was a virgin?"

Zach nodded, feeling even worse now that she had said it. "Yes." He had handled this situation all wrong, let his feelings for her carry him away. He wasn't used to being out of control; the knowledge that he could be, under any circumstances, was hard to handle.

Sunny shrugged, as if it were no big deal. "Well, now I'm experienced," she said cavalierly.

Zach released a frustrated breath. "That's not funny, Sunny," he said, chastising bluntly, as guilt flooded him again. He had taken something precious from her, something that couldn't just be given back. And that in turn made their relationship even more complicated than it already had been. And dammit all, she had known that.

"Look, Zach, it had to happen sometime," she reassured him gently, her fingertips stroking his chest, making him want her all over again.

Zach scowled. Once again, Sunny was too naive for her own good. She should have had a real marriage, and until he'd come along she'd held out for just that, he admitted grimly to himself. But maybe it wasn't too late. "I'll make it up to you," he said softly, realizing he was more of an old-fashioned guy than he'd thought. "I promise."

Sunny's face flamed, as she mistakenly took his concern for her as rejection. Before he could correct her misimpression, she pushed away from him and sat up, dragging the sheet over her breasts. Her eyes flared with a temper she was working very hard to subdue.

"Listen, Zach," she lectured. "I never asked you to hold the key to my chastity belt. In fact, if you want to get technical about it, the way things were going...you had every right to expect we'd eventually make love."

No, Zach thought, he hadn't. He'd only hoped.

"This doesn't have to change anything," she persisted willfully.

He shook his head at her, amazed at her innocence once again. "You're wrong, Sunny," he said gently. "What happened between us just now changes everything." Because she had given her heart to him—body and soul—and now their marriage was a real one in every respect.

SUNNY VAULTED from the bed, the sheet draped about her like a long white toga. She couldn't believe he was filled with ambivalence about the most wonderful thing that had ever happened in her life. Now reality was sinking in. "Why does it have to change everything, Zach?" she asked coolly, slipping out of the bedroom and into the galley. She bent to extract a can of icy lemonade from the cooler and settled into the booth. Outside, the storm had passed. Only a gentle rain remained.

"Because it does," he insisted.

Sunny watched as Zach wrapped himself in his robe. His straight ash blond hair all tousled, his face shadowed with just a hint of evening beard, he had never looked sexier. "You don't have to feel guilty," Sunny said quietly. *You don't have to feel trapped.*

"How do you expect me to feel?" He got himself a cold soda and joined her in the tiny vinyl booth. Maybe if he got her talking, he'd find out how she was feeling about all this, too.

How about pleased, instead of horrified, Sunny thought, taking a long sip of her lemonade. But seeing that wasn't about to happen, at least not today, she shrugged. "Sexually satisfied, I guess." She turned to look at him and said slyly, "You were satisfied, weren't you?"

Zach swore, the heat of his embarrassment and chagrin moving from his neck into his face. He looked heavenward for his answers. "Why me?"

Sunny grinned, enjoying his discomfiture. It wasn't often the tables were turned. "That's no answer, Zach," she answered with an inner steeliness she couldn't begin to feel.

He leveled his glance back at her. "You know I...was," he said thickly.

"How would I know?" she shrugged. "It's not like I've had a lot of experience in the area, you know," she said dryly.

"Yes, I know," Zach drawled.

His blue eyes glimmered as if he had every intention of making her his again. But not before they'd talked, Sunny surmised.

"And now that we're on the subject—" he captured her bare legs beneath the table and shifted them onto his lap "—why haven't you had a lot of experience?"

She closed her eyes and didn't answer. Zach stroked her legs, from ankle to knees. "You wanted the first time to be with your husband, didn't you?" Not just someone who was pretending to be your husband, he thought, then swore inwardly again. Maybe if they'd agreed to stay married and make their union a lasting one, it would have been different. But they hadn't. So he'd have to convince her...to make their marriage last, not just for a short time, but forever.

Sunny ignored the tingles starting beneath his caressing fingertips. She stared at the tabletop, beginning to get embarrassed now despite herself. "I waited because I wanted it to be special," she admitted reluctantly, not meeting his eyes.

"And it wasn't," Zach interrupted, with a self-effacing sigh.

She glanced up. He was so hard on himself sometimes. "What makes you think that?" she asked curiously. For her, it had been very special.

"Because it just wasn't—that's all." At least not special enough to make her want to stay married to him, Zach thought, his determination growing. "But it could be," he said as he took her hand and pulled her out of the booth.

"Zach—"

He wrapped her in his arms and pressed his lips into the fragrant softness of her hair. "Sunny, we can't leave it like this."

Sunny shook her head. Through the opening of his robe, she could see the suntanned column of his throat, muscled chest and crisp golden brown hair. She pressed the flat of her palm on his skin. Confusion clouded her eyes. "I haven't the slightest idea what you're talking about."

Zach's heart thudded heavily beneath her hand.

"Precisely my point," he said dryly.

Sunny sighed and ran her hand up to his shoulder. "I think what happened was wonderful." She couldn't ever remember feeling as loved as she had when he'd made her his for the very first time.

Zach traced the swell of her breasts, above the tucked-in sheet. "You're right—it was great—but it could have been a lot better."

Sunny tilted her head back to better see his face. Zach was half teasing, half serious. "What do you mean?" she said softly, wondering all the while if he was falling in love with her as hard and fast as she was with him. Had it not been for the crazy way they'd gotten together, would he have been this open with her?

Zach raked his fingers through her thick red-gold hair. "If I'd known you were a virgin, I would have gone about it very differently," he said gently. "You'll just have to trust me on the fact that your introduction to lovemaking could have been a lot more ... um ... enticing. Fortunately," he teased, sifting his hands through her hair and giving her a decidedly sensual glance, "it's not too late for me to make amends."

But did he love her? she wondered. Or was he just trying, once again, to right another wrong? Until she knew for sure... "Zach, I—I'm tired," Sunny fibbed.

Just as he'd suspected, Zach thought, she already had one foot out the door again. He quirked a brow. "Too tired to see what else you've been missing all this time?"

Sunny hesitated. He would have to point that out. She had always been curious about what it would be like to have a lover. She studied his face, liking the rapt adoration she saw there beneath his overriding concern, loving even more the idea of making love with him all night. Though she couldn't imagine it being any more enticing ...

The temptation to find out what else she'd been missing was great, but so was her anxiety, and right now, she felt she and Zach were poised on the brink of either total happiness or disaster. "If I'd known this was what we were going to be doing on this boat, I would have brought some champagne with us," Sunny groaned. "Anything to help me relax."

He massaged her shoulders. "You are a little tense."

"Now that I'm thinking about what's going to happen, Zach, I'm getting nervous about it again."

Zach paused. He dropped his hands. "Then maybe we should put it off a little while," he suggested.

Sunny wavered between relief and disappointment. It seemed he was full of surprises today. One minute possessive, the next willing to let her go her own way.

"The rain's stopped," he continued affably. "We could take a break, go on deck and enjoy the sunset. After all, we've got all weekend to perfect our love-making skills."

Sunny sighed. She had her reprieve. She just wasn't sure she wanted it.

"TRUST ME, Sunny. There's nothing like sleeping under the stars."

Sunny stood motionless beside Zach. She'd waited for him to make his move, and he hadn't. Not during dinner. Not after. Not at all.

She looked at the foot-high solid white Plexiglas railing on top of the houseboat. "At least we don't have to worry about falling off in our sleep. But if it rains, we're in trouble."

"It's not going to rain," he said firmly.

"If my memory serves me correctly, that's exactly what you said before," Sunny remarked sagely.

"Yeah, well, this time it wouldn't dare," Zach said as he dragged the mattress up on top of the sun deck, atop the houseboat cabin. Together he and Sunny spread out blankets, sheets and pillows. He took her hand and tugged her down beside him. They were both clad in menswear pajamas, thick cotton socks and deck shoes. "Trust me, Sunny, this will be a great place to spend the evening."

"I admit it's cozy up here," she said, looking up at the stars and the moon overhead. "Kind of like camping out, only better."

"It seems we're the only two on the lake tonight, doesn't it?" Zach said.

"Probably the only two people fool enough to be out here after that storm we had this afternoon," she joked, settling back on the pillows, her hands folded beneath her head.

"Yeah, well, there's something to be said for storms," Zach said softly, drawing an imaginary line down her middle.

"Oh, yeah?" Sunny teased, as the warm rain-scented air blew over them.

"The storms in your eyes are magnificent to see." He reached over and began to undo her pajama top.

She inhaled a shaky breath. "Zach—"

"Relax, Sunny."

He turned her on her side; she was nestled against his warmth, so she could see the gentle, serious light in his eyes.

"We've got all night." He cupped a hand behind her head and kissed her slowly, deliberately. "And I intend to take my time."

Where before there had been passion and urgency, there was only tenderness and care. He undressed her one button, one snap at a time.

He lingered over her breasts and her thighs and every sweet inch between. He kissed her repeatedly, languid kisses that were as intimate as his caresses. He kissed her in ways that revealed his soul. And she loved him back, starting shyly, growing more and more bold. Spearing her hands through his hair, across his shoulders, down his torso to his thighs, she offered him whatever he wanted from her, whatever he needed. And this time, she took, too.

She was lost in him. She was in love with him. And she needed him. Oh, Sunny thought, surging toward the outer limits of her control, how she needed him ... needed this ... wanted to feel loved ... and so incredibly cherished.

ZACH PARKED in the driveway and cut the motor. Wordlessly he snapped off his seat belt and hers, dragged Sunny across the bench seat of his pickup into his arms and settled her on his lap.

"What are you thinking?"

She sighed wistfully, not sure when she had ever felt so content or so loved. "That what happened this weekend changes everything."

"For the better," Zach agreed as she laid her head on his shoulder. He chuckled softly. "Living with you and not loving you was getting to be damn hard."

Sunny stroked his chest with long, soothing strokes. She sensed he was delaying going back inside for the same reason she was. "Now that we're home again, Zach—" she began.

Reading her mind, he touched a fingertip to her lips. "I want to share your bed every night. Or you can come to mine. It doesn't matter, as long as we're together."

Sunny drew a deep breath. She could feel the thundering of his heart beneath her palm. "So this wasn't a fling?"

Zach shook his head. "We're married partners involved in a full-fledged love affair." He paused, studying her face in the moonlight. "How does that set with you?"

It frightened and thrilled her all at once. "I think I can live with it," she said cautiously, curling her fingers in the fabric of his shirt. *As long as it doesn't ever end.*

Zach smiled, his happiness as potent as hers. "So it's settled," he said, running a possessive hand down her spine. "From now on, we'll be together every night."

"Yes," Sunny said softly. They would make love endlessly and sleep wrapped in each other's arms. And for once, she wouldn't worry so much about the future.

Zach's eyes darkened passionately. He cupped the back of her head and kissed her gently. Within seconds, they were both trembling.

"If we stay out here much longer, we're going to end up giving the neighbors a show," he teased.

Sunny grinned, unable to imagine a time when she wouldn't want to make love with him over and over again. "You always did look cute wrapped in nothing but a chamois loincloth," she murmured.

"Not to mention what you do for a red-and-white checkered tablecloth," Zach quipped back, as they drew apart reluctantly and she slid off his lap. "But if we're going to play Nature Walk dress-up, we'll have to do it inside the house this time."

He hopped down and circled around the truck to help Sunny down. She paused as her feet hit the ground, frowning as she caught sight of her Land Rover. She was sure she'd left it parked out back. It was now next to the house and sporting a huge red ribbon across the top. Sunny glanced at Zach. He was grinning complacently. "Do you know anything about that?"

Zach gave her an aw-shucks look. "I just might." He set down their bags and took her hand. "Let's go see."

"It smells like . . . pine!" Sunny said in unmitigated delight, once they'd opened the door and the interior light had come on. "And is that new carpet on the floor?" Her vehicle looked brand-new again inside.

"Yep."

"Zach, how did you manage this?"

"I enlisted a chemist friend of mine from Vanderbilt. He was able to treat the leather seats, but he feared the carpet would be a lost cause, just as I did, so I had the local garage rip it out and replace it with new."

"I can't believe it!" Sunny stuck her head inside the truck. "No skunk smell! I can drive my Land Rover again!"

Zach pulled her against him, so they were both still facing her vehicle and touching front to back in one long, tensile line. "No more bad memories?" he said, clasping his hands in front of her.

Sunny grinned up at him. "From now on, Zach, the only memories we have of skunk are the funny ones."

"Good. Now there's only one thing left to do," he said, scooping her up into his arms. Holding her against his chest, he strode toward the front door of her house.

"And what is that?" she asked, her heart thudding heavily against her ribs.

Zach winked at her. Pausing on the steps, he bent his head to give her a slow, leisurely kiss that sent fire sizzling through her in waves. "Make some new memories," he said.

Chapter Eleven

Hearts in Armor

"That must have been some vacation you and Zach took," Gramps said slyly. "You haven't stopped glowing all morning!"

Sunny flushed. She had been afraid it would show. But she couldn't help it. She had never felt more loved in her life, even if Zach hadn't yet said the words.

"He even carried her up the steps and through the front door upon their return, honeymoon-style," Matilda added, as she joined the conversation around the coffeemaker.

Sunny's eyes widened in surprise.

"Sorry, honey," Matilda continued, "but the two of you are the talk of the town. It does all our old hearts good to see you two young-uns looking so happy."

"Especially mine," Gramps said. "I knew Zach was the man for you all along."

Sunny had known it, too; she just hadn't wanted to admit it to herself. And she wasn't going to confide it to Gramps, either, at least not yet. "I'm glad you all are so happy," she said dryly, "but now it's time to get back to business. Has Chuck Conway arrived yet?"

"He's supposed to be here any minute to work with me on the new computer system," Matilda said.

"Please ask him to stop by my office and see me when he's through," Sunny said. "I've got a few questions of my own to ask him."

"Will do," Matilda said.

"Well, I'm going to check out the new designs and then go fly-fishing," Gramps said.

Sunny kissed his tanned cheek. "Enjoy yourself. You've earned it."

Gramps grinned back at her. He patted her shoulder affectionately. "Thanks, I will."

Sunny spent the rest of the morning in her office. Around noon, Chuck Conway appeared in her door. The thirty-year-old software engineer was wearing a gray herringbone suit that looked brand-new. An overabundance of after-shave clung to his jaw. "Hey, Sunny," he said as he breezed in. "Heard you wanted to see me."

"Yes, I did, Chuck. Come on in."

He shut the door behind him and strolled closer, running a hand through his slicked-back brown hair.

Sunny noted he appeared more self-conscious than usual.

"So what's up?" Chuck asked, his eyes glued to her face.

Sunny got up from her desk and motioned him closer. Chuck's voice carried and she didn't want anyone overhearing what she was about to say. "Do you think Matilda can handle that new system you installed for us?" she asked.

Shoving both hands in his trousers, Chuck shrugged. "I think so."

Sunny bit her lip. "You're sure we don't need something simpler?" she insisted worriedly.

He shook his head. "Something simpler wouldn't meet your needs, Sunny. Therefore it'd be a bad business decision."

She sighed and looked into Chuck's eyes. She wanted him to understand. "Making Matilda feel incompetent because she can't understand the complicated system you installed is bad business, too."

"You could always hire someone else to help you out with it," he said. "Someone younger. And assign Matilda to something else."

"No, I don't think so."

"Well, then." Chuck grinned as if she'd given him an unexpected Christmas gift. "I guess I'll just have to come up here every day and see you all until we get things squared away," he said, stepping even closer.

Again he looked at her funny.

"Is everything okay?" Sunny asked, puzzled by the way he was peering at her.

"It will be," he said. "Once I get this over with."

Before Sunny could guess what he was going to do, he had bear-hugged her around the middle. Knowing he was about to kiss her, she shoved her elbows into his ribs. His legs got tangled up with hers.

He tripped and they both went sprawling, with Sunny crashing sideways into the display of untreated wood samples. She gasped as the soft pine splintered beneath her weight, ripping her panty hose and embedding in her skin.

"What the hell's going on in here?" George came crashing into the office. "Sunny, are you all right?"

George stepped over Chuck to get to Sunny. He helped her to her feet.

She looked down at her burning thigh and groaned. "Oh, no."

"YOU WANT to tell me how you got this injury?" Zach said.

"Not particularly," Sunny replied breezily. She kicked off her shoes, rolled down her panty hose. Hiking up her skirt, she carefully climbed up on the examining table and rolled onto her side. "However, if you must know, I crashed into a display and fell on some wood."

Zach narrowed his eyes at her, his proprietary male side coming to the fore. "It's not like you to be clumsy."

How well Sunny knew that. But she hadn't expected Chuck Conway's five-year crush to suddenly manifest itself in a pass today. In retrospect, she could see she never should have called him at home after-hours, asked him to meet with her alone. All had been "clues" he had added up the wrong way.

Both irritated and embarrassed to find herself in this situation, she propped her head on her hand and grumbled, "Can't you hurry it up with the medical treatment? I need to get back to the office."

Zach treated the area with antiseptic. "I'd love to oblige you, but these splinters are going to take time to get out."

Sunny groaned. She couldn't think of a more ridiculous and humiliating position to be in, though Zach didn't seem to mind the work, or the fact that she'd had to take off her panty hose and hike her skirt nearly to her waist.

"So. How has your day been?" she asked, in an effort to keep her mind off what he was doing.

"Busy. I saw fifteen patients this morning, and I have a nearly full appointment book this afternoon, too."

Sunny winced as he removed a splinter and put it in the basin beside him. "Word's spreading."

"You can say that again," Zach agreed. "And not just about my skills as a physician." He paused to take out two more splinters, then gave her an interested glance. "Do you know people saw me carry you across the threshold last night?"

Sunny blushed, even as she noticed how good he looked in a white lab coat. "It was mentioned to me, too."

Zach's face split into a grin. "Everyone thinks we're on a honeymoon," he reported, his voice dropping to a sexy whisper.

"It feels that way to me, too," she said. Which was another reason she didn't want to spoil the current romantic mood with stories about Chuck and his hopelessly misguided attempt to kiss her. In this instance, what Zach didn't know wouldn't hurt him, she decided.

"I'm glad to hear that you feel that way," he said. Finished taking out the splinters, he treated the area with antiseptic cream.

"Why?" Sunny asked, watching as he expertly bandaged her thigh, then ripped off his surgical gloves.

Zach leaned over her, caging her against the examining table. "'Cause this honeymoon of ours is not over yet," he warned in a voice that made her heart pound all the harder. "Not by a long shot," he promised as he pressed his lips to hers and delivered a long, leisurely kiss.

Sunny was trembling when he finally lifted his head. She knew if they hadn't been in the clinic, he would have made love to her then and there. With effort, she marshaled her thundering pulse.

"I've got a class tonight after work, but I'll try to be home as soon as I can after that. Maybe by around seven-thirty," she promised.

"I'll be home as soon as I can, too," he told her, looking as if he were anticipating their reunion after a day spent apart every bit as much as she was. "Unfortunately, tonight is my night to make house calls on the shut-ins in the area, so you'll probably beat me home. But not by much if I have anything to do with it," he vowed softly.

"WHAT A beautiful baby," Zach said, as he finished examining Heidi Pearson later that same day. He had stopped by their house at the end of his house calls to save Rhonda-Faye and George a trip to the clinic. Now, inside their warm cozy home, which was brimming with kids, he was glad he had.

"I didn't think physicians were supposed to be partial to their patients," Rhonda-Faye said, bundling her newborn daughter back up in swaddling clothes.

Zach winked at Rhonda-Faye and stepped over one of Toby's toys. "I won't tell if you won't."

"Are you going to have babies with Sunny anytime soon?"

Good question, Zach thought. Maybe it was time to start a family.

"Hi, Doc." George came into the room.

"Ready to get those stitches on your forehead out?" Zach asked.

"Sure thing." George sat down in the chair Zach indicated as Rhonda-Faye slipped from the room, Heidi in her arms. "Sorry about the way I acted when Rhonda-Faye went into labor," George said. "I get a little crazy whenever our kids are born."

"So I heard." Zach grinned.

"Think you'll do the same?" George asked.

That, Zach didn't know. "I consider myself to be pretty calm during medical emergencies," he said finally.

"You're pretty calm about what happened to Sunny today, too," George remarked casually, surprised.

"You mean about the splinters?" Finished taking out the stitches, Zach cleaned his scissors and tweezers thoroughly with alcohol.

"Yeah, the way it happened and all," George said matter-of-factly.

Once again, Zach had the feeling Sunny was deliberately shutting him out. Ever so casually, he replaced his scissors and tweezers back in his medical bag. Time to go on a fishing expedition. "What did you think about what happened?" Zach asked, folding his arms in front of him.

"Well, I know Sunny didn't see it coming, but I knew he'd make a pass at her eventually."

Zach froze. "What was the guy's name again?"

"Conway. Chuck Conway."

The same guy she had talked to on the phone. "I've never met him," Zach said benignly. "What's he like?"

George ran a hand over his hair. "Harmless. Nerdy. Kind of clueless, if you know what I mean."

I'm beginning to. "So he's had a crush on Sunny for a long time?" Zach asked.

"Yeah. I don't think she was even aware of it. You know how Sunny is. She doesn't see stuff like that, but me and the other guys did."

Then how come you didn't stop it? Zach tamped down his anger deliberately. "How was she at the time it happened?" Zach asked, then explained, "She was calm when she got here. She had kind of shrugged it off."

George rubbed at his jaw thoughtfully. "I think she was shocked, but she didn't take offense. She just figured it was a misunderstanding, that Conway read her wrong, which isn't surprising, 'cause like I said, the nerd's clueless."

Sunny should have told me this! Zach thought.

"Ticks you off, doesn't it, Doc?" George stared with a provoking grin.

"Well . . ." Zach shrugged. "She is my wife."

"So naturally you feel protective of her," George continued affably.

"Naturally."

"Want my advice?"

Zach knew he was going to get it anyway. Maybe George knew how to handle a situation like this. "Sure," Zach said.

"A woman likes a man to take charge. This Chuck Conway incident, for instance. Sunny would probably never admit it in a million years, but she probably secretly wanted you to go all jealous on her and get upset and so forth."

Zach didn't have to pretend to feel that way. He was upset. And Sunny was going to know it!

"I CAN'T DO THAT!" Sunny told her marriage class.

"Honey, with a body like yours, you've got nothing to hide," Gertie said.

"Right. It's the rest of us that ought to be worried about greeting our husbands at the door covered in nothing but plastic wrap!" Matilda said.

"Particularly me, since I just had a baby," Rhonda-Faye said, patting her ever-flattening tummy. "And can't participate in the...um...follow-through yet."

"Rhonda-Faye, you have permission to delay this particular exercise until your physician gives you the okay to resume relations," the instructor said.

"Seems fair," Matilda commented.

"Speaking of fairness," Sunny interrupted. "Can't we amend the lesson a bit?" she asked. "Forget the plastic wrap and just dress in a suggestive manner and greet our husbands at the door? For instance, I have a beautiful negligee I got as a wedding gift that I haven't even worn—"

"Sunny Carlisle, why ever on earth not?" Gertie demanded.

Sunny blushed. "I was waiting for the right occasion."

"That was for your wedding night!" Gertie said.

"Well, I uh—"

"What she's trying to say is she didn't need it on her wedding night," Matilda broke in, in an attempt to save the day. "And even if she had put it on, that cute young husband of hers probably would've taken it right off... so why not save it for later, when the love life got a little dull? But so far there hasn't been time for it to get boring, right, Sunny?"

Sunny knew she was blushing to the roots of her hair. She sank down in her chair, covering her red face with her hand.

All the women laughed. "I think you hit the nail right on the head," Rhonda-Faye drawled. "Not that it's surprising. Sunny and Zach are both young and gorgeous, and at that age where their hormones are in full bloom. They'd have to be monks not to appreciate each other, especially in this newlywed phase."

"Back to my question," Sunny said as she doodled aimlessly on the notepad in front of her. "Couldn't I just greet Zach at the door in that negligee? Maybe with some champagne?"

Maybe if she did, he would forget to ask more questions about how she'd gotten those splinters in her thigh earlier today, Sunny thought.

"All right, Sunny, if you'd be more comfortable, you can wear a negligee instead of plastic wrap. But the rest of the assignment still stands. And we want a full report during the next and last class!"

SUNNY LOOKED at herself in the mirror and shook her head. The negligee she was wearing was made of pale peach silk. The bodice was low-cut and clinging, the fabric blissfully opaque.

She wore matching peach silk mules and a matching peignoir. Had it not been for the weekend they'd spent together on the boat, she would have felt ridiculous. But now that they were lovers, she felt nothing but anticipation. Last night, making love to Zach in their bed, in their own home, had been wonderful. Tonight, Sunny decided as she poured two brimming glasses of champagne, would be beautiful, too.

A car engine sounded in the driveway. That had to be Zach, and he was right on time.

Picking up the glasses of champagne, Sunny switched on the stereo and floated to the front door. Looking through the front screen, she did not see Zach. Instead she saw two people she had never met. She hadn't a clue who they were, but from the looks on their faces they apparently knew just who she was.

"You must be Sunny Carlisle," the woman said.

Sunny set down the champagne. She drew the edges of her peignoir together, a little embarrassed to be caught in a nightgown during the dinner hour. "And you are?" she asked, already afraid she knew.

"Nate and Maxine Grainger, Zach's parents." Zach's father held out his hand.

Sunny shook it warmly.

"He didn't tell me you were coming," she said nervously, glancing at the wood-paneled station wagon in her driveway.

Zach's mother smiled. Petite, blond, she was dressed in a long-sleeved knit blouse, denim wrap-around skirt and sneakers. She had the same Nordic good looks and blue eyes Zach did. "That's because he didn't know," she said kindly.

His dad, who was as tall and fit as Zach was, added, "We wanted to surprise him."

"Well, you've certainly done that." Sunny opened the screen door to let them inside.

"But why did you come here looking for him?" she asked. Zach had not told his parents he was married as far as she knew. "I mean, I—we—"

Zach's father held up a hand. "No need to pretend, Sunny. Maxine and I don't want to pry, but we might as well tell you the secret is out of the bag. We found out on Saturday, when we called the clinic looking for him. The answering service operator told us he was out of town with *his new wife.*"

"Naturally—" Maxine picked up the story where Nate had left off "—we were shocked to find out he had married without even telling us. So we decided to drive on up here today, after we finished teaching school, and find out for ourselves what was going on."

Sunny blushed. She wished Zach were there to take the heat right along with her. "I don't know what to say," she murmured. This was *so embarrassing.*

Fortunately she was saved the trouble as Zach turned his pickup into the drive. She pointed behind the Graingers and smiled cheerfully, unable to completely disguise her relief. "There's Zach now."

"He has a lot to answer for," Nate said, pulling a pair of glasses out of the pocket of his seersucker shirt.

Zach bounded out of the truck, his medical bag in hand. He grinned wickedly as he caught a glimpse of Sunny's outfit, then bounded across the yard and up onto the porch, where he hugged his mother and father warmly. "I guess you know," he said finally.

"I guess we do," Maxine said.

The trio looked at one another with so much affection it made Sunny tingle.

"I was going to tell you," Zach said eventually.

"Why didn't you?" Maxine said.

Sunny held her breath. She didn't know why exactly, but she hoped he would not tell his parents their marriage was a fake and that they were forced into it by the well-meaning members of the close-knit, but old-fashioned, community.

Zach shrugged and wrapped a possessive arm around Sunny's shoulders. "Isn't it obvious? I wanted to keep my beautiful wife to myself. Besides," he continued in a more serious tone, "I thought you might object to my hasty wedding."

Maxine leveled an admonishing finger at her son. "The only thing I object to is you not inviting us to the wedding."

Zach shrugged and said with a careful honesty Sunny applauded, "It was one of those affairs that was thrown together at the last minute."

"I see." Nate regarded his son with a combination of sternness and love.

Sunny felt a lecture coming on. "I think I'll go upstairs and change," she said, eager to take off the negligee.

"I REALLY AM sorry that you got the news about my marriage to Zach the way you did," Sunny told Maxine as the two of them whipped up a salad for dinner.

"No need to apologize, dear," Maxine said as she rinsed the lettuce leaves and then placed them in a colander to drain. "I think I know why Zach didn't tell us. He probably thought we'd make a fuss, which we would have. And he probably felt he couldn't handle the emotional aspects of it."

"I don't understand," Sunny said slowly.

Maxine drew a breath. "Because of Lori. He took her death very hard. We all did, and since then big family gatherings and holidays have been hard on the three of us. Zach's wedding would have been bittersweet. He probably thought—erroneously, I might add—that he was protecting us by not including us."

Sunny didn't know about that, but it did explain Zach's distance from other people and the walls he had put up between himself and the community.

"He loved Lori a lot, didn't he?" Sunny said, wishing Zach would talk about his kid sister's death with her as freely as his mother did.

Maxine nodded. "The two of them were extremely close. I don't think they had any secrets from each other." Maxine teared up, and she had to pause to wipe her eyes, as she confessed thickly, "Zach sacrificed so much of his own life, just to be with her. And then he took her death very hard. I don't think he has really let anyone close to him since. Oh, he has plenty of friends, both male and female, but I think there's been a fence around his heart ever since then. Until you, of course. You must have really thrown him for a loop."

"I think that goes both ways," Sunny said. He had certainly thrown her feelings into turmoil. She had never been so simultaneously happy and sad as she was right now.

"Perhaps we should talk about something else," Maxine said.

Sunny nodded. She and Zach would work this out. It would just take a little more time for him to get his life back on track. When he did, he would see there was no reason for him to keep from getting close to those around him.

Sunny sliced carrots with a vengeance, aware she wanted Zach as she had never wanted anyone or anything else. How she wished theirs were a normal marriage.

"You and my mom were in the kitchen a long time tonight," Zach said as he and Sunny got ready for bed.

Sunny slipped a long white nightgown over her head and sat down on the bed. As she brushed her hair, she lifted her eyes to his. "She told me about Lori, Zach."

Somehow, he had figured that was the case.

He kept his glance level. "She did."

"She thinks Lori is the reason you never married until now."

Zach tensed. "She's probably right," he said in a matter-of-fact tone. Clad only in pajama bottoms, he eased down beside her. "Lori's death took everything out of me that I had to give. I had enough left over for patients, but that was all."

Sunny clasped his hand tightly in both of hers. "Tell me about her."

Zach stared down at their entwined hands. Talking about what happened to Lori made his gut twist, but he knew it was past time he started talking about his loss. There was no one he wanted to confide in more than Sunny.

Marshaling his inner strength, Zach looked into Sunny's eyes. The compassion and understanding he saw there gave him the courage to continue. "Lori was two years younger than me. From as far back as I can remember, it was always my job to protect her. And I did until she was thirteen, and she got leukemia. She was sick off and on for the next twelve years. She suffered through three all-too-brief remissions before finally dying of the disease two years ago. I was her cheerleader, her patient advocate. I did everything I could think of to help her get better, including a lot of research on my own." He sighed wearily. "I was so sure we could beat the cancer if we went after it together."

"I suppose she had all the newest treatments?"

Zach nodded, recalling with difficulty how hard it had been on his sister. And through it all, she'd been such a trooper, never complaining, never giving up, even at the bitter end. His eyes welled with tears; determinedly he blinked them back. "I even gave her a bone-marrow transplant," he said thickly. "It didn't help." He gripped his hands in front of him until the skin around his knuckles turned white. "Nothing did."

"Is that why you became a doctor?" Sunny asked gently, covering his hands with the warmth of hers. "Because of what happened to your sister?"

He nodded slowly. "I went to the hospital with her every time she needed chemo. The more I learned about her disease and what they could and couldn't do for her in terms of treatment, the more I wanted to know."

Sunny put her hairbrush aside. "Your mom said you sacrificed much of your own life to be with her."

"I don't think it was such a big deal. Although—" Zach grinned, recalling what a stir that had caused "—I think Mom's still mad at me for skipping out on my senior prom."

"You didn't go?"

"Lori was sick and was in St. Jude's hospital. How could I have had a good time, knowing what kind of shape she was in? So I canceled and spent the night at her bedside."

Sunny released an unsteady breath. She was looking at him as if he were some sort of a saint, Zach thought uncomfortably.

When in truth, all he could focus on was the fact that he had failed his sister.

"I wish I had known her," Sunny said finally.

Funny, Zach could imagine the two of them to-gether. It was a poignant vision. "I do, too," Zach said softly. "I think she would've liked you.

"And she would've especially liked," Zach added, simultaneously blinking back tears and laughing lightly, "the way you don't hesitate to give me hell when you think I need it."

Sunny's lips curved in a teasing grin. "Let me guess," she deadpanned. "Lori gave you hell, too?"

Zach nodded, the good memories crowding out the bad once again. "You bet she did. Lori read me the riot act all the time, as any good kid sister would. She wanted to bring me up right she always said. And in her opinion, Mom and Dad were both too soft on me."

Sunny smiled. "You really have a loving family."

Zach nodded, shifting his grip so that he held both of Sunny's hands in his. He knew how lucky he was, never more so than now. "I'm glad you like them," he said. "They've taken to you, too." Just as he had known they would. "My mom said she really enjoyed talking with you tonight. And speaking of talking to someone," Zach said, reminded of what he had been waiting all evening to find out. "What's this I hear about Chuck Conway putting the moves on you to-day?" He was still surprised by the amount of jeal-ousy that information had evoked in him.

Sunny flushed. "How did you hear about that?" she moaned, looking as though she wanted to die of embarrassment.

"Never mind how I found out," Zach said sternly, for once glad the efficient grapevine in Carlisle existed. "Why didn't you tell me Chuck was the reason for your splinters?"

"Because I was afraid you'd react like a jealous husband," Sunny said, rolling her eyes.

He felt like a jealous husband. It didn't bother him as much as he would've expected. "I don't want him putting the moves on you," Zach said firmly, meaning it. The next time he wouldn't let it go by without incident.

"It won't happen again," Sunny told him confidently as she slid beneath the covers and lay back against the pillows.

Zach slid in beside her, but delayed turning off the light. "How do you know it won't happen again?" he said, studying her upturned face.

Sunny shifted onto her side and regarded him smugly. "Because I told him what no one else had bothered to report to him—that I am married now."

Zach shifted onto his side, too. "How could he not have known?"

"Chuck doesn't reside in Carlisle, Zach."

"Even so—" he began.

"I don't know." Sunny waggled her eyebrows at him teasingly. "Maybe he isn't as into gossip as everyone else, including you, in this town is."

"Very funny."

Sunny lifted a hand in warning. "Just don't go getting any ideas about fistfights on my behalf."

Zach grinned and began to unbutton her chaste white nightgown. "Only if you put that peach negligee on again."

"Zach!" She swatted at his hands.

He pushed her hands away and kept unbuttoning. "I mean it. My blood has been boiling ever since I caught a glimpse of you in it."

She nudged his thigh with her knee and whispered hoarsely, "Your parents are just across the hall."

Zach grinned, not the least bit upset. "They think we're newlyweds." And these days, he felt like one. "They won't mind."

Zach bent to kiss her. Her lips parted for him and she uttered a soft little groan in the back of her throat.

"What if they hear us?" Sunny said, worrying out loud.

Zach slid a hand inside her gown to cup her breast, and felt her nipple bud against his palm. "Then you had better be quiet, hadn't you?" he whispered back, dropping his palm lower, exalting in the way her soft curves heated beneath his touch.

"Mmmmm." Sunny moaned again, arching up against his questing fingers, even while she initiated a few clever moves of her own. "Gramps was right," she teased. "You *are* bad news...."

"You ain't seen nothing yet," he promised, and then set about divesting her of her nightgown and making her his all over again.

"If I'm going to be naked, you're going to be, too," Sunny declared, unsnapping his pajama bottoms.

"Sounds good to me." Fierce desire already swirling through him, Zach covered her with his body. Dipping his head, he kissed her thoroughly until she was feeling the same way and her lips were hot and wanting beneath his.

"Oh, Zach, you make me feel so good," Sunny murmured. She nestled against him, softness to hardness, their caresses flowing one into the next, until there was no ending, no beginning, only a sweet continuum of unrelenting pleasure that drove him on and on.

Slowly he filled her, and she received him, arching at the pleasure, taking him deeper and deeper inside.

Feeling as if he were drowning in her softness, the sweet solace her lips offered, he moved with her, molding the length of his body to hers.

They came together, the power and the emotion of the moment stunning him, leaving him lost and free all at once.

He had not ever imagined it could be like this. Sunny drew a passion and tenderness from him that he never would have dreamed possible. And she did it without half trying, Zach thought, holding her close and drinking in the soap and perfume scent that was uniquely her.

He knew this was love. But was it marriage? He sensed they would both find out soon enough. Whatever happened, he was not letting her go, not giving up. Life was too short, too precious, for them not to be together, he decided fiercely. The only question was, how was he going to convince Sunny of that? How was he going to make her believe that they needed to live their lives free of gossip and community pressure?

As strange as it was, she actually liked the interference.

"Zach?" Sunny said sleepily, cuddling close.

"Yeah?" He brought the covers up around them, his heartbeat settling down to a contented purr.

"I'm glad you told me about Lori."

"I'm glad, too." He stroked a hand through her hair, a wave of tenderness washing over him. "It felt good to talk about it. Maybe because I never do."

And it had brought them closer, Zach thought with a satisfied grin as he curled an arm possessively around her.

If everything continued to go right, the two of them might get past their shaky beginning and make a real marriage of this yet.

Chapter Twelve

I Don't Fall in Love So Easy

"How's the poison ivy, Slim?" Zach asked at the graduation party for Sunny's how-to-be-happily-married class.

"Lots better, thanks to the medicine you gave me," Slim said with a wink. "Though I gotta admit it's the first time I've ever had poison ivy where the sun don't shine."

Zach laughed softly. Slim was nothing if not honest. "Guess you appreciated the side benefits of having your wife take this class, hmm?"

"Didn't you?" Fergus asked, coming up to join the group. "It certainly brought a lot of zip to my marriage with Gertie, and that was something...well, let's just say after thirty-one years of marriage, I didn't expect it."

"What about you, Doc?" George asked, joining the men at the punch bowl. "Did this class lend any zip to your marriage or were you so deep in the honeymoon phase that you didn't even notice?"

It would have been hard not to notice Sunny in that peach silk negligee, Zach thought, the memory of the night they had spent in each other's arms after his parents had left still vivid in his mind. "Since I've never been married, that'd be kind of hard to know," he said.

"Got a point there, Zach," George agreed. He cast a fond look at his wife, who was cradling their new baby in her arms. "All I know is that I wouldn't trade Rhonda-Faye for any woman in this world, I love her and the kids so."

Zach knew how George felt. He didn't want to trade Sunny, either. And that had given him second thoughts about leaving Carlisle.

"WHAT DO YOU MEAN my transfer request was put on hold a long time ago?" Zach asked the clerk in charge of the outreach program incredulously.

"We had a call from the governor several weeks ago, right after your request came in. He said he had talked to your local sponsor, Augustus Carlisle, and that you had changed your mind. Something about you marrying his granddaughter Sunny and settling in there right fine."

"So you're telling me he canceled my request *for* me?" Zach asked.

"Well, yes." The clerk paused. "Does this mean you want to reinstate it?"

"Yes! No! I don't know," he said. "I'll have to get back to you." He hung up and charged out the door of the clinic. He and Augustus were going to have it out once and for all.

Unfortunately Augustus wasn't home, and he wasn't fishing, according to his housekeeper. He was at the factory with Sunny.

Zach thought about waiting, then decided this confrontation couldn't wait. Augustus had crossed the line for the very last time.

Zach stormed into the factory. Sunny and her grandfather were in the showroom with a group of prospective buyers. Sunny left her group and crossed to his side.

"Is everything okay, Zach?"

He didn't want to upset Sunny. This wasn't her fault. Like him, she knew nothing about it. "I just need to talk to your grandfather. Clinic business." Which was true, as far as it went.

Sunny turned. "Gramps, Zach needs to talk to you." With a dazzling smile, she rejoined her group. "Now, where were we?"

"What's so all-fired important?" Augustus said.

"This conversation needs to happen in private," Zach said grimly.

Gramps took a good look at his grandson-in-law's face. "No problem," he said smoothly. "We'll use my office."

They strode in silence to his office, a cubbyhole next to Sunny's executive-sized haven. Gramps shut the door behind him. He immediately faced off with Zach. "Let's have it, greenhorn."

"I just talked to the outreach office in charge of rural physician assignments."

"Oh." Augustus had the grace to look chagrined.

"Yes, 'oh'," Zach said heavily. "I notice you're not denying you called the governor?"

"I talk to him regularly. We're old friends."

"You put a halt on my request."

"What did you expect me to do? You had just married my granddaughter."

"I don't care," Zach said evenly. "That wasn't your call to make."

"I don't know what you're so all-fired upset about." Gramps was incensed. "It worked out in the end, didn't it? You and Sunny are as happy as can be."

"That's not the point," Zach roared, exasperated beyond belief. "You trapped me into marrying Sunny and then you manipulated me into staying well past what was necessary under the circumstances."

"Now you're talking nonsense," Augustus growled.

No, Zach thought, he wasn't. In fact, judging by the increasingly guilty look on Gramps's face, there might be even more to it than he'd originally realized.

"Who exactly was on the selection committee that brought me here?" Zach asked cordially.

Gramps blanched and didn't answer.

"Sunny was on the selection committee, wasn't she?" Zach pressed.

"So what if she was? A lot of other people were on it, too."

"Did she get to choose me, or was it more a group effort?" he asked.

"I don't know what you're talking about," Augustus returned hotly as he picked up a fishing lure from his desk. But he wouldn't meet Zach's eyes.

Barely able to believe how stupid and gullible he'd been, Zach stalked nearer. He planted his hands on Gramps's desk and leaned across it. "Are you denying that Sunny went through the files that were sent here, picking and choosing among the candidates?"

Gramps shrugged and looked all the guiltier as he tied a piece of line to a feather. "I admit she helped us try to find a good match by reading through the résumés right along with the rest of us. But that was all she did, Zach."

It was more than enough. His jaw clenched.

"The idea of us choosing you for some evil purpose is just ludicrous," Gramps continued.

Was it? "So why didn't you choose a woman physician?"

"Because we live so far out in the country, it made more sense to choose a man!"

"And I was the one Sunny was most interested in!" he said, guessing slyly.

"You had a fine résumé," Gramps retorted, exasperated. "A fine education."

Zach recalled how impressed Sunny's parents had been by his education background; he wondered if that had factored into the decision, too.

As he realized how well and easily he'd been duped, it was all Zach could do not to slam his fist into the wall. "So you admit you all lured me to the community with the idea of me marrying your granddaughter in mind!" he shouted back triumphantly.

"I wouldn't say we had the idea of marrying you two right off," Gramps said hotly.

Zach read between the lines, his experience with the wily old man telling him there was a lot more to this than what appeared at first glance. "But you did expect me to keep company with her!" he asserted baldly.

"Well, why not? The two of you were both well educated and among the few young unmarried people in this town. Sure, I hoped she might date you when she finally got to know you!!''

"Let's be honest," Zach said grimly. "This was all a plot from the beginning, wasn't it? You lured me to Carlisle so that your granddaughter would have a husband. You used me to keep Sunny here in Carlisle, make her happy and give you a grandson." Zach didn't know why he hadn't put it all together sooner. Now that he had, he felt like such a damn fool. "Well, the game's up!" he said furiously. "I'm through being caught in a snare!"

SUNNY STOOD outside Gramps's office, her face going alternately white and red. Reminded of how she and Zach had really gotten together, she wanted to die. There was no love involved here, only passion. She had been fooling herself into thinking there was.

Bracing herself for the battle to come, she opened the door and stepped inside.

Zach looked at her. "I heard everything," she told both men, her expression stony with resolve. "Including the fact that Zach thinks he's been had."

"Can you blame me for feeling I walked into a trap?" he asked.

Hell, yes, Sunny thought. But not about to let herself sink to the shouting level of the men, she shook her head and shut the door quietly behind her. "You're right, Zach," she said sweetly, moving closer to join them. She looked at him innocently. "It's all been a nefarious plot. I paid those skunks to trail me and made sure you were driving on that particular country road, on that day, at the precise time I was checking out the reforestation of that select slice of company-owned land. Then—and this was the truly difficult part—I somehow convinced those skunks to follow me, knowing all the while that you were bound to see me in danger and pull your pickup to the side of the road, leap over the fence in a single, soundless bound, creep up from behind and scare the life out of me and get us both sprayed with skunk. Then, not content with that, devious woman that I am, I made sure you were driving a brand-new truck that you would of course refuse to let us ride in. I had nothing in my knapsack but a tablecloth, and you nothing but a chamois—''

Zach silenced her with a look. "All right, all right. So maybe the skunks were an accident, but they played right into your grand plan," he asserted.

Sunny looked heavenward. "Right, Zach. I wanted to get caught by my grandfather and two policemen with me in nothing but a tablecloth and you in a chamois. I wanted to be humiliated beyond belief."

Zach's mouth tightened. Sunny knew she had finally gotten through to him; he knew how ridiculous he sounded, even if he wasn't about to forgive her or Gramps.

"You didn't object to marrying me!" Zach thundered.

"No," Sunny said very quietly as tears of frustration sparkled in her eyes. "But I should have. It was a bad idea."

"You two were happy the past few days," Gramps interrupted. "And you can't deny you were!"

No, Sunny couldn't deny that the past few days had been among the best of her life. But that was apparently where it stopped. "We were deluding ourselves!" she said miserably, blinking back her tears. "We got caught up in the honeymoon aspect of things, but we weren't dealing in reality. The reality is we got married for all the wrong reasons. It took us a while, but we have finally woken up. Now that we have, I want out, and so apparently does Zach. So you have your wish. I'll start divorce proceedings tomorrow. Gramps will call the governor back and ask him to expedite your transfer request. *Won't you, Gramps?*"

"Of course, Sunny."

"And in the meantime, Zach, you can sleep at the clinic! Now, is everybody happy and satisfied?" she asked with icy control. She knew she wasn't! Not waiting for an answer, she turned on her heel and stormed from Gramps's office.

"Sunny—" Zach started after her. He caught up with her in the central bull pen. Disregarding the company employees gaping at them, she shrugged off the grip he had on her arm. "Leave me alone, Zach. We have nothing further to discuss."

"The hell we don't!" He clamped a hand on her wrist and directed her into her office.

There was a murmur of approval and excitement behind them. Sunny ignored it. She waited until Zach had shut the door behind them and released her. "I don't know what this is going to prove," she said, moving away from him defiantly.

He rounded on her. "I want to know why you married me."

She regarded him stonily, feeling as if her heart were encased in a block of ice. She let out a long breath and looked away.

Hands braced on his waist, he eyed her implacably. "You regret it, don't you?"

"Yes. Because what's happened here today has made me realize that the marriage was a mistake. It was unnecessary. And I knew it in my heart all along." Sunny's lower lip trembled as she forced herself to admit. "But I wanted to be with you, so I let them bully and talk me into it. Just as you did," she conceded miserably.

Zach nodded his understanding grimly. He pushed impatient fingers through his hair. "So what now?"

Sunny knew they were at a turning point. This time she was determined to make the right decision, to behave as an adult rather than a lovestruck teen.

She moved to the window and stood looking out at the Tennessee mountains she'd come to love. "I knew when I moved here that I was not going to put my energy into lost causes anymore. For years, I did everything positive to win my parents love and affection, and as you saw for yourself, they still barely know I'm alive. That isn't going to change. I'm not going to beat my head against the wall anymore, trying. And I'm not going to torture myself like that again. Especially when I know through my easy but newfound relationship with Gramps and everyone else in Carlisle that unconditional love does exist."

"Unconditional love, my shoe. He pressured you into marrying me, Sunny." And he could not forgive her grandfather for that.

Sunny raised her chin. "Yes, he did, because he was old-fashioned and hopeful enough to think that was the best thing for both of us to do under the circumstances. But had I stood up for myself and said no and meant it, he would have stopped pressuring me. He would not have stopped loving me then any more than he did just now when I read him the riot act.''

Zach shook his head in silent censure of all that had happened. He felt as miserable as she did. "I can't live here anymore."

Sunny sighed. She was not surprised. Zach had wanted out of Carlisle almost from the moment he'd arrived. "I figured as much," she said tightly.

He gave her a long look, his expression stony. "So what about us?" he asked grimly.

If he had shown her the least sign, indicated he was in love with her or wanted to try again, Sunny would've moved heaven and earth to be with him. But he didn't. Instead he acted as though this were a business agreement in need of resolution, and nothing more. Well, she thought wearily, perhaps that was all it had ever been to him. A business deal, with passion thrown in. Initially that was all it had been with her, too. She'd just had the bad sense to fall in love with him.

"What about us?" Sunny echoed dispassionately. *Tell me it's not too late, Zach,* she pleaded silently.

He stared at the floor for a long moment. A muscle worked in his cheek. Finally he looked back at her, the expression in his eyes bleak and unforgiving. "You said you wanted to file for divorce?" he stated, very low.

She saw the guilt in his eyes, the regret. And suddenly she knew that he had only stayed as long as he had, tried as hard as he had, because he'd wanted to make a success of his career in Carlisle and thereby guarantee his future as a physician. "Yes, I'll handle the expense and paperwork involved in a divorce,"

Sunny said, knowing she couldn't bear this heart-
break for one more second. "You won't have to do
a thing, Zach. You're free to go. Your life is your
own again."

Chapter Thirteen

Life Is Too Short to Love like That

"I can tell from the heartbroken looks on your faces that you've heard the news, too," Sunny told her marriage class, as they gathered in Rhonda-Faye's diner after hours.

"It's true, then?" Rhonda-Faye said as she served strawberry sodas to everyone. "You and Zach are calling it quits?" She was incredulous.

Sunny put on her bravest face. "He thinks I brought him to Carlisle to trap and coerce him into marrying me, so I cut him loose."

"Oh, surely he knows that isn't true!" Matilda said, appearing as upset as Sunny and the rest of the group.

Sunny stirred her soda disconsolately. "The circumstantial evidence is running against me. He knows I went through the profiles of the various physician candidates with Gramps and said Zach's was interesting."

The ladies grinned as if that were proof Sunny had been head over heels in lust with Zach even then. "You can't fall in love with a picture," she said dryly.

"But you can fall in love with the flesh-and-blood reality of an intriguing picture," Matilda said slyly.

Sunny sipped her soda. It was delicious, but she could take no pleasure in it. "Whether I'm attracted to Zach isn't the issue here. He is through being used and wants out of Carlisle. Like it or not, my marriage is over," she reported dejectedly.

The ladies exchanged concerned looks.

Rhonda-Faye eyed Sunny seriously. "All I know is that a marriage takes work, even for the most in-love couple on earth."

"Rhonda-Faye's right. The two of you gotta break each other in," Aunt Gertie said. "And have a few tiffs as you settle into matrimony. That's all that's been going on between the two of you. You had a tiff. You told him to take a hike, more or less, exactly as you should have, under the circumstances. Now it's time to tell him that you forgive him for his stupidity—and that it's okay to come back to you. We've all done the same thing with our men, haven't we, ladies?"

The group nodded unanimously.

Her expression both serious and helpful, Matilda elaborated on Gertie's advice. "Sacrifice is the key here, Sunny," she said. "For you and for Zach."

"And let's not forget compromise," Gertie added. "You can't have a marriage without both those ingredients."

"You can't have a marriage without love, either," Sunny said morosely, staring into her strawberry soda. If Zach had really loved her, he would've known that she had never meant to trap him into marriage, and he never would have left.

"Oh, now, honey. Zach loves you!" Gertie said.

Rhonda-Faye nodded vigorously in agreement. "I've never seen a man so silly with it. He's head over heels in love with you."

He's head over heels in lust with me, you mean, Sunny thought. And they were not the same thing. "Then how come he never said so?" she asked the group belligerently.

"Maybe because of the way your marriage started— at the end of a shotgun," Rhonda-Faye said softly.

Sunny didn't want to admit it, but Rhonda-Faye had a point. Zach had been forced into this more or less against his will. The only way he'd been able to salvage his fierce pride and self-respect was to tell her repeatedly that he refused to give in to the social pressures being exerted on him. Admitting he loved her probably was tantamount to failure, at least in his view. At the very least, it was proof he'd lost his independence and done what everyone else had predicted would happen all along.

"Try reading his face instead of his lips," Matilda advised.

"Oh, I don't know," Aunt Gertie teased, "you can tell a lot from the way a man kisses, too. Tell me true, Sunny. Does Zach kiss you like he means it?"

And then some, Sunny thought wistfully.

"If there's love in his kiss, there's love in his heart."

No matter how much she tried to forget them, Aunt Gertie's words stayed with her the rest of the impromptu meeting. Zach did kiss her as though he loved her, she thought. And there had been other signs he cared about her, too. The way he'd fixed up her car, for instance, helping to get rid of the skunk smell. Then there was his jealous reaction to Chuck Conway's pass at her. The way he had comforted her after her parents' visit and protected her during the storm.

So what if he hadn't come right out and said the words? Neither had she. Yet she had felt his love. And would still be feeling it if she hadn't overheard his conversation with Gramps.

Was it too late for a second chance? She hoped not. All she had to do was swallow her pride, find Zach and try one more time to work things out. She knew that if she didn't, she would always regret it.

She left the diner and went straight to the clinic.

To her disappointment, the front door was locked. A Closed sign was in the window. Beneath that was a printed notice announcing that another doctor would be arriving to take Zach's place at the clinic just as soon as the state agency and the local selection committee could arrange it. Zach's truck was nowhere in sight.

Sunny blanched. Was it possible he had already left? Moved out and on?

Despondently she returned to her house. Her hopes rose as she saw his shiny new pickup sitting in her drive, then fell again as she noted the bed of the truck was filled with his belongings. Either he'd come home to her—which seemed damn unlikely, considering how they had left things between them—or he had just stopped in to talk legalities with her before he left town.

Aware her legs were shaking, Sunny stepped out of her Land Rover. She moved toward the house, the first few steps taking all the willpower she had. And that was when she saw him, slouched on the steps of her front porch. In jeans, dress shirt and tie, he had never looked more handsome. Or more unapproachable. She eyed him cautiously, unsure of his mood.

Zach unfolded himself and stood with a determined, lazy grace that quickened her heartbeat.

"About time you got home, woman," he said softly, curling his thumbs through the belt loops of his jeans.

Sunny stared at him, not sure whether to laugh or burst into tears. She knew only that she had never felt more tense or uncertain or full of bittersweet anticipation in her life. And Zach, damn him, was to blame.

Pride stiffened her shoulders. "Since when did you turn into John Wayne?" she returned, regarding him with a coolness she couldn't begin to feel deep inside.

"Since I was cornered by Slim, Fergus, Gramps and George." He swaggered laconically down the porch steps like the hero in a Western movie, not stopping until he towered over her and they stood toe-to-toe. His blue eyes were shrewdly direct as they locked on hers.

"*They* think I handled you all wrong."

Sunny's lips curved sardonically. Whether he wanted to admit it or not, they had formed their own marriage-counseling service for men, although it was a little less organized. She folded her arms in front of her and adopted a contentious stance. "Well, it'll warm your heart to know that the women in the community think I've handled you all wrong, too."

Zach braced his hands on his waist. "Is that a fact," he drawled.

Sunny nodded, her temper soaring as all the things they had said to each other at their last meeting came rushing back to hit her square in the heart. Honestly, how could Zach ever have thought she had set him up for a shotgun wedding? Shouldn't he have known instinctively she was not to blame? And where did he get off acting all macho now? As if she were the one to blame!

"Furthermore," Sunny continued loftily, drawing her own line in the sand, "I think they're right," she fibbed, twisting things around for the sake of her own argument. "I think I should have kicked you out weeks ago!"

"Okay," Zach said, "that's it. I've heard quite enough for one evening." He scooped her up in his arms, carried her across the porch.

"Creating yet another scene for the neighbors to see?" she asked sweetly.

He shrugged as he entered the house. "It's not my fault there's nothing this entertaining on TV."

"Zach, I'm warning you. I am in no mood for games."

He paused just inside the threshold. Still holding her in his arms, he cradled her against his chest, the passion he'd always felt for her gleaming in his eyes.

"I don't want to play games, either, Sunny. I want to make things right."

Sunny's heart pounded at his proximity, but she refused to sacrifice her pride, when she'd already sacrificed so much. "By divorcing me?" she asked coolly.

"By loving you," Zach corrected as he slowly set her down so her feet touched the floor.

Sunny saw the intent look in his eyes. It kindled her own fires. Needing to clarify things for her sake, to make sure he was there because he loved her, she stepped back, announced defiantly, "Zach, I can't go back to having an affair with you, even if we are legally married."

Framing her face with his hands, he tilted it beneath his. "How about being my wife, then, in every sense?"

Unable to move without risking closer contact, Sunny held her ground. She wanted so much for them—a happy marriage, children and everlasting love. She wanted him to want them, too. "And how long is this offer good for, Zach—as long as you stay in Carlisle?"

"No, Sunny, as the vows said," he told her, blocking her in place, when she would have tried to march past him once again, "for as long as we both shall live."

Sunny swallowed. She stared at his tie, her pulse racing; she was unwilling to admit how much just the thought of letting him go disturbed her. It appeared it was about to happen. "So you're still planning to leave Carlisle, then?" she asked, a little sadly, aware her mouth was dry and her palms were damp and that she'd never had so much at stake in her entire life.

"I received my official transfer." He gestured toward his truck matter-of-factly. "As you can see, I even packed up and got ready to leave town."

Unable to help herself, Sunny moved another half step closer, so they were standing just inches apart. "What stopped you?" She knew the answer she wanted to hear.

"You." Eyes darkening seriously, he dove his hands into her hair. "I realized I not only didn't want to leave, Carlisle, I couldn't." His voice caught. After a moment in which he stared long and hard at the horizon, he forced himself to go on. "The thought of a life without you is unbearable, Sunny."

Her heart leapt at what he had just admitted. She tipped her head up to his. "Because of the passion between us?" she asked slowly, knowing that if they were going to be together again, their relationship had to be real, and it had to be right.

"I admit I love the way we make love, Sunny, but that's not what is keeping me here," he said hoarsely. "I'm here because you hold the key to my happiness. I gave you my heart without ever knowing it. Just as you gave yours to me. I love you, Sunny," he said huskily. "And I always will."

Nothing he could have said would have pleased her more. "Oh, Zach." She wrapped her arms about his neck and kissed him sweetly. "I love you, too," she whispered emotionally. "So very, very much." They kissed again, putting everything they felt into the caress. "But I want you to be sure this is what you want," Sunny said tremulously at last.

"It is. Although I regret to admit it's taken almost losing you to make me realize it. I know I've been unfair to you, to everyone." He paused and shook his head in silent admonishment. "Lori's death took so much out of me that I wasn't sure I had any love to give. And for a very long time I didn't want to find out if, or even when, that would change. And I sure as heck didn't want to fail anyone I cared about again," he finished fiercely.

Sunny hugged him hard as the rest of her doubts melted away. "Oh, Zach, you didn't fail Lori," she reassured him gently. She leaned back against the warm cradle of his arms to gaze into his face. "You did everything you could for her."

Zach's fingers tensed, then relaxed again as he talked openly about his pain. "Only it wasn't enough, and it damn near killed me. I didn't want to fail you, too." His eyes sobered. "But I realize now the only way I could fail you is by walking away."

Sunny swallowed. They had one more bridge to cross. "What about feeling trapped?"

Zach gave her a long, steady look and admitted on a rueful sigh, "The only trap I fell into was putting a fence around my heart. Coming to Carlisle, meeting you, set me free again."

Euphoric relief surged through her. Against all the odds, despite all the meddling, she and Zach had a future together. She had never felt more complete. "Big talk there, fella," Sunny teased, laying a hand over his heart. Beneath her fingers, she felt its strong, steady beat, and knew her world had righted once again.

"Yeah, but it's from the bottom of my heart," Zach said in a rusty, trembling voice. "All these how-to-be-a-proper-husband hints from the guys must've sunk in," he offered with a teasing wink.

"Must have. They're working on me, at any rate." Sunny wrapped her arms around his waist and leaned in close, savoring his warmth and his strength and the essence that was him.

Zach lifted the veil of her hair and kissed her exposed throat. "Does this mean you forgive me?"

"Guess so," Sunny quipped as her heart soared. Her eyes danced as they met his. "You're a hard man to stay mad at."

"Now, why is that, I wonder," Zach drawled, looking incredibly happy and content, too. He kissed her full on the mouth, a long, slow kiss that made her tremble.

"Maybe because I love you, too," she confessed. Surging into his embrace, she guided him back to her for another soulful touch. Finally they drew apart. "Zach?" Sunny said, her knees so weak and trembly she could barely stand. She knew where she wanted all this to lead.

"Hmm?" Once again sweeping her up into his arms, he carried her up the staircase.

"About our marriage—" she began.

"It's a real one, in every sense," he confirmed, striding unhurriedly down the upstairs hall. "Truth to tell, I think it has been for a long time." He put her down gently, then followed her down on the bed, kissing her long and slow and deep, drawing on all the power and the wonder of their love. Sunny had never been happier, or more replete.

"Zach?" she said breathlessly after a while, as she began to work off his tie and he undid her buttons.

"Hmm?" He slid a warm palm against her skin.

"About that baby we've both talked about in the hypothetical, the one we both want someday but have been afraid to plan on." Sunny caught her breath at what he was doing and looked into his clear blue eyes. She saw the promise of the future. "How about making it a real possibility?"

Zach paused, his face aglow with delight. For the first time, they really did have it all. "Sunny, love, you read my mind."

HART'S DREAM is one such story.

At first they were dreams—strangely erotic. Then visions—strikingly real. Ever since his accident, when Dr. Sara Carr's sweet voice was his only lifeline, Daniel Hart couldn't get the woman off his mind. Months later it was more than a figment of his imagination calling to him, luring him, doing things to him that only a flesh-and-blood woman could.... But Sara was nowhere to be found....

#589 HART'S DREAM
by
Mary Anne Wilson

Available in July wherever Harlequin books are sold. Watch for more Heartbeat stories, coming your way—only from American Romance!

HEART9

ANNOUNCING THE

PRIZE SURPRISE SWEEPSTAKES!

This month's prize:

L-A-R-G-E—SCREEN PANASONIC TV!

This month, as a special surprise, we're giving away a fabulous FREE TV!

Imagine how delighted you and your family will be to own this brand-new 31" Panasonic** television! It comes with all the latest high-tech features, like a SuperFlat picture tube for a clear, crisp picture...unified remote control...closed-caption decoder...clock and sleep timer, and much more!

The facing page contains two Entry Coupons (as does every book you received this shipment). Complete and return *all* the entry coupons; **the more times you enter, the better your chances of winning the TV!**

Then keep your fingers crossed, because you'll find out by July 15, 1995 if you're the winner!

Remember: The more times you enter, the better your chances of winning!*